THE CHRONICLES OF
Bria Twon

THE CHRONICLES OF
Bria Twon

EARTHA GATLIN

AHTRAE
PUBLISHING, LLC

Dedication

To the wind beneath my wings:
Demond, Paris, Jasmine, Jada, JaKobe

Acknowledgments

I would like to acknowledge God, my mama, and my daddy, without whom I wouldn't be here; to my children for putting up with the real me and loving me anyhow. You all know I only want the very best for you. To my grands, you two already know; my then husband whoever he was at that time who encouraged me and said you are smart and intelligent and can do anything you put your mind to. Even to the one who said if you would devote as much time to developing yourself as what you spend catering to others you could have written five books, finished school sooner—bachelor's, master, and a doctorate, 10 degrees, and so on and so on. (Okay, I'm overexaggerating, but I'm a writer, right? That's what we do.) You get my point and know who you are. I appreciate you too. Thanks for your flagrant way of saying I could do this. Side note: It wouldn't be me if I didn't add some humor, y'all.

But on a serious note, I must give kudos to Joyce, my friend and confidante who read my manuscript years ago and kept it confidential. Thanks for reading the draft, putting it in a binder and sending it back to me. I still have that marked-up copy. Thanks also for saying to me upon learning of my retirement, "So what's next? You gonna finish that blankety-blank book?" You always believed in me. I appreciate you. Also, thanks for giving and introducing me to Hope.

To Hope, thanks for your support and friendship. I appreciate you.

Thanks to my girl Nik for listening to my dreams and pushing me to fulfil them. You are a black girl who rocks and haven't even scratched the surface of your full potential. I hope to inspire you. Again, thank you, and can't wait to celebrate your new movement. Yes, I put it out there, so you have to achieve it. Remember our slogan, *Don't talk about it. Be about it.*

Thank you to my adoptive-surrogate mother Henrietta Dotson-Williams for all your love and support. You're another one who knew my dream, read my draft years ago and never said a word to others. You encouraged me to write and move forward. I love and appreciate you.

Thank you to Mrs. Kimberla Lawson Roby for your patience, kindness, and willingness to sit down with me to share your expertise *and* for accepting my calls to answer questions. I was floored and touched when you spoke and referenced me as a "writer." Thanks for not being selfish with your craft. Thank you, Chandra Splond Sparks, my editor. You are the bomb.com. Now, I will admit, some of your comments had me questioning why I thought I could do this. I thank you for always being there when I needed you and most of all for your professionalism and frankness.

To Lisa (Woo), you are an inspiring and encouraging old soul. Thanks for being real. You knew my journey and still supported me. Thank you. To my sister LaWanda, thanks for keeping me grounded. You never let a sista forget where she came from. Your love and support is captivating. I love and appreciate you. Shout out to Rob and Shanda. Thanks for loving my babies. I know it's tough, but somebody's gotta do it. Seriously, I thank you both for all the love and support and for being a great addition to our family.

Last but certainly not least, my ride or die, my A-one from

day one. Girlfriend, we have been through the storm. Who would have ever thunk it? Remember that episode at the bank? Too funny. I will never forget it (inside story). From hoopties to stakeouts (another inside story), Louisiana—I thank God the miles couldn't keep us apart. Trips to New York, Charlotte, Martha's Vineyard, the Bahamas, Jamaica, and Dallas, and so much more to come. Thank you for being my friend and riding this out with me. I love and appreciate you for your unconditional, unwavering, nonjudgmental friendship and sisterhood through this journey. We've come a long way, girlfriend. They ain't seen nothing yet.

Special thanks to *all* my other friends, relatives (aunts, uncles, first cousins/cousins (Janice/Bruce), nieces, nephews, sister/brother-in-laws), church family, and colleagues too many to name who poured into my spirit, who loved and supported me... You know who you are. I appreciate you. Without you, this book would not have been possible.

Chapter One

SABRIA TWON, AFFECTIONATELY CALLED BRIA by family and close friends, was born in 1960 and raised an only child by Beatrice McKellar, a single parent.

Bea, as she was called by family and close friends, was born in 1935. Bea's mother, Mama McKellar, was a devout Baptist woman while PaPa McKellar, her father, was just the opposite. He believed in God, but he did not participate in the Baptist traditions nor did he attend church services the way Mama McKellar did. Instead PaPa McKellar believed a man's place was working and seeing that his family was taken care of, so most of his time was spent working at the paper mill in what was known as Coosa Pines in Childersburg, Alabama.

Usually on his days off, which would be Saturday and Sunday, he purchased homemade corn whiskey from one of the neighboring sellers and enjoyed drinking with his buddies.

Most of what Bea learned about family and relationships she got from her parents.

Back in those days, it wasn't uncommon for a young girl to become pregnant, but when things like that did occur, the girl was made to marry the father, or someone other than the natural father would marry the girl so no disrespect came to her or her family.

On other occasions when no father stepped up, the grandparents would raise the child. The latter was the case with Bea. She married once, but not the father of her children. By the time she had given birth to her first child, Bea was divorced. It wasn't until later in life that the children knew anything about Bea's first husband.

True to the norm of those times, Bea's southern mother and father insisted on taking and raising the children. Bea's first child was born and reared in the south and had always lived with Bea's parents. The remaining three were born in the Midwest. Then, when things got tough for Bea, she sent two of them down south to be reared along with the first, so ultimately all the children except for Bria were reared in the South.

According to Mama McKellar, Bea had ways like her father—they both liked to drink and cuss a lot. Back then Bea didn't consider PaPa McKellar's aberrant drinking and behavior a problem and never considered herself an alcoholic. She believed it was the normal way of life since that was all she knew, and she claimed it was just socializing and having fun—until her drinking started affecting things personally like missing work, paychecks, and ultimately losing employment.

In the 1950s, Bea migrated from her southern upbringing in Alpine, Alabama, to the north—Rockford, Illinois. At that time, Rockford had been officially named one of the largest cities in Illinois, second to Chicago. In those days, Rockford was a major industrialized hub and home to many nationally known manufacturing companies. Many men and women moved to Rockford from the south to claim their so-called fortunes and to have a better life for them and their families.

In the early years around 1955, long before Bria's birth, Bea had been up north, as the Midwest was called by southerners, for quite some time and had begun to meet men who admired her southern beauty, innocence, and personality. Even though Rockford had become very industrialized during that time, Bea got a job as a seamstress at Bella's, a small dress boutique in downtown Rockford. She learned to dress very well. Bea would wear heels and dresses daily and appeared classy and carried an allure of sophistication. Many men shopped at Bella's Boutique for unique gifts for their spouses. Some of the men Bea encountered were married; others were not. Bea loved the attention.

Bea was the only African-American employee at Bella's during that time. When African-Americans patronized the store, Mrs. Younger, the owner, always made sure Bea's presence was known.

"Hello, sir, and how may I help you today?" Mrs. Younger smiled at the astute-looking gentleman as he peered through the showcase.

"Yes, please, allow me to introduce myself. My name is Lee

Cox. Well, I know it's rather late in the day and you're about to close, but I sure would appreciate it if I could get a hand at picking something very special for my wife. It's our anniversary," Lee said.

"No rush, Mr. Cox. We're happy to help. We understand how it is with those last-minute purchases, especially with our gentlemen clientele. Now you just go ahead and take your time. As a matter of fact, why don't I get my salesclerk Bea to help. She has marvelous taste and an eye for just the right accessory," Mrs. Younger said. "Bea, can you come out here, dear?"

Bea entered the storefront wearing a tweed maroon-and-vanilla houndstooth woven jacket and solid maroon form-fitting skirt. Bea's silk nylons adorned her shapely calves, which flexed well with each step of her black leather pointed-toe pumps. Lee Cox could barely maintain his composure, but the feeling—the look in his eyes upon first glance at Bea—just about said it all.

Bea always carried a natural elegance and subtle sophistication when she entered a room. She stood five feet, six inches tall, weighing 134 pounds. Since working at Bella's, she had adapted well to coordinating fashions with accessories. She had impeccable taste in clothes and shoes. This was just like any other day at the store. She always prided herself in her appearance.

"Yes, ma'am?" Bea said.

"Bea, would you mind helping this fine gentleman? He's shopping for an anniversary gift for his lovely wife. I told him I knew you would be able to find just what he's looking for. Would you mind, dear? Go ahead, and I'll finish up the paperwork in the back. Just take your time, dear. I'll be in the back office," Mrs. Younger said.

"Sure, Mrs. Younger. You know I would love to help," Bea answered.

Bea and Lee Cox seemed charmed by each other. Bea chose a bejeweled brooch for Mrs. Cox, but in Lee's mind, he chose Bea and had become distracted by her beauty and grace.

Chapter Two

"GOOD NIGHT, MRS. YOUNGER. I'LL see you tomorrow. Have a good evening." Bea pulled the door up and ran into the alley to her regular spot under the awning on the back of Bella's receiving dock to catch her cab home.

Whew. It's raining hard tonight. I hope I don't mess up my hair, Bea thought. Simultaneously, bright lights and the sound of a horn in the distance caught Bea's attention.

"What in the hell is going on?" Bea spoke to herself, barely audible.

"Would you like a ride?" Lee asked, speaking to Bea through the half-rolled glass.

"My mama told me not to ride with strangers, sir," Bea

flirted, batting her naturally long eyelashes.

"I don't consider myself no stranger, young lady," Lee said.

Lee Cox had a body shop on the southeast side of town. Bea lived with her brother, Earl, on the southwest side of town between Lee's shop and Bella's downtown. Earl had moved to Rockford after returning from the armed services by way of Alpine, Alabama. Bea had always been very close with her brother, so it came as no surprise when she informed her mother and father she would be moving from Alpine to Rockford too.

After that first night, it had become routine for Lee to close up shop around the same time Bea was to close up Bella's. Lee started wining and dining Bea, showing her a gentlemanly view of a man she had never known.

Lee fancied buying and presenting Bea with gifts of real gold and small diamond jewelry. He once purchased Bea a black faux sable full-length fur coat with a matching hat and muff. Lee and Bea would take weekend getaways to the nearby town of Loves Park and frequented a resort called House on the Rock between the cities of Dodgeville and Spring Green, Wisconsin, located two hours from Rockford.

Bea was having the time of her life. Occasionally, when Lee was not able to get away, Bea would frequent the Legion, a local nightspot owned and operated by a group of African-American veterans. In those days, the Legion was a place people of color frequented and took pride in. The spot was located in their neighborhood on the southwest side of Rockford near downtown. Most of the businesses in that area were owned and operated by African-Americans. There were a couple of mom-and-pop soul food restaurants and about three different nightclub spots where the local musicians played. Bea loved to dress up and go out dancing.

Bea was intrigued by Lee and all his attention toward her. She was equally impressed because no other man had ever made her feel significant. Bea viewed the jewelry and fine clothes as a sign Lee cared for her. Those things combined made her feel like a million dollars as she would often say. Lee treated Bea like a queen. He told her how beautiful she was, and he loved her smile, her flawless skin, her poise, and her sense of humor. For as often as Bea and Lee were together, no one would have known Lee was actually married to someone else. Bea didn't question him about his wife or how he managed to spend so much time with her. She just enjoyed every moment of their being together. Secretly, Bea envisioned she and Lee would be together forever.

Lee continued to greet Bea after her shift at Bella's, all the while Bea kept the affair from her boss Mrs. Younger.

Until one day.

"Bea, I noticed you've been getting a ride lately. Have you met someone, dear?" Mrs. Younger asked.

"Oh, um, yes, ma'am. Just a fella I met through my brother," Bea answered.

"Well, I hope, he's nice, dear. A young woman like you deserves to meet someone nice," Mrs. Younger said. "Don't let any man use you, dear. You know men will do that, especially to young beautiful girls like yourself. You know what happened to my baby sister Faye. She met a man, he claimed to love and care for her, then come to find out he was married. Poor Faye never was right after that. Just be careful, Bea. My husband, Bobby, and I really do care for you. Since you've been with us, you're like family. I sure wouldn't want to see anyone hurt you, dear."

"Oh, don't worry, ma'am. I won't let nobody hurt me," she politely answered.

"Well, you go on. I'll lock up tonight. Bea, think about what I said, dear," Mrs. Younger said.

"Good night, Mrs. Younger," Bea said. She felt like Mrs. Younger knew she wasn't being upfront with her but tried not to show it.

Bea was caught off guard by what Mrs. Younger had said, but it wasn't her first time being warned about her relationship with Lee. Bea's brother had often questioned the integrity of Bea's relationship with Lee given they were spending so much time together. But Bea just shrugged it off as Lee being just a friend.

"You know you should be ashamed of yourself, Beatrice. Momma would have a fit if she knew you was carrying on with that married man," Bea's brother, Earl, said.

"But Momma happens not to be here, now is she? Last time I checked, Momma was in Alpine not Rockford," Bea snapped.

Since moving to Rockford, Earl had been more than a big brother to Bea. He acted like a father figure instead. Bea loved their brother-sister relationship, but highly resented Earl's superiority role and would not bite her tongue to let him know.

Momma and Poppa McKellar had entrusted him to care for her, and Earl had vowed not to let them down. Momma McKellar had a special bond with her son, but the relationship with Poppa McKellar was a bit strained. Poppa believed his son was gay and had encouraged him to go to the army believing that would make him straight. In those days, being gay was not openly discussed in public so most families would try to keep it confidential to their immediate family or not discuss it at all. But Poppa knew and so did Momma. When Earl returned from the army, most of Earl's friends were homosexual men. In fact, no one ever spoke about Earl's sexual orientation—not even Bea. Earl was often described as a handsome man. He was six foot six, had a chiseled face and was muscularly built, yet he never introduced a girlfriend to his parents.

Bea and Earl rented a small three-bedroom brick bungalow in Rockford. Bea didn't care what anyone thought about Earl. He was her brother, and she would do anything to protect him. Bea and Earl might have their differences of opinion, but Bea did not stand for anyone talking bad about her brother. Earl had a great personality, and most everyone who knew him loved him.

No matter the bickering about Lee and Bea's relationship, Earl had always been there for Bea. Even when the worst happened, Earl came through for Bea. Earl tried to warn Bea about her immoral behavior and the negative outcome of dealing with a married man, but she wouldn't listen. Bea remembered vividly the night she told Lee she was pregnant.

Bea and Lee had just ended what to Bea was hot and passionate lovemaking, Lee had drifted off to sleep, and Bea sat up in bed, twirling the covers between her fingers. Bea was pondering whether to let Lee sleep longer while watching the ticking clock. By ritual, Lee would always wake up at 10:30 p.m., go to the bathroom, wash up, and leave by eleven. He didn't say why, but Bea always suspected it was because he needed to get home at least by twelve to his wife. During the week, Bea accepted Lee having to leave her early, but on Saturday nights, she had a problem with it. She knew Lee needed to allow time to go home to his wife and get some rest so he could get up early for church on Sunday to serve as deacon.

The clock read 10:23. Bea ran her fingers lightly over him. She loved watching the dark chiseled backbone of the man she loved. Lee was approximately five-six, medium dark and very solidly built with broad shoulders and a cut stomach for a man in his early thirties. He was ten years Bea's senior. Bea slightly nudged Lee.

"I'm late this month, Lee," she informed him.

"Late? Late for what, baby. What time is it?" Lee asked.

"I'm late for my cycle."

Lee rolled over and away from Bea. "I know you're not talking about what I think you are talking about."

"I think I might be pregnant, Lee."

"Hell no. You gon' have to do something about that, Bea. You know my situation."

"Your situation? What the hell is your situation? You never talk about your situation. The only situation I know about is this situation, muthafucka," Bea snapped back.

"See, there you go. Now calm down, Bea. I'm married, girl. What will I tell my wife, Ellie Lou?" Lee pleaded.

"You know what, Lee? You, Ellie Lou, and all the rest of you muthafuckas can kiss my black ass. You weren't thinking about telling Ellie Lou a damn thing when your black ass was over here fucking the shit out of me, were you? Get the hell out of my bed and out of my life, man. I guess all good things must come to an end," Bea said.

Bea always had the tendency to cuss and throw a fit—her

mother, Margie Anna, would say Bea was contrary just like her father. No matter how much Bea loved Lee, she wasn't about to let any man mess her around. Occasionally Bea's mouth got her in trouble. She would often lash out in anger before rationally thinking. This was one of those times.

Lee rolled out the bed, searching for his belongings.

"Don't worry about me or what's in my belly. We don't need a damn thang from you," Bea said.

Lee continued dressing, foregoing the usual wash up, and left.

Bea never asked Lee for any financial support for their daughter, Bria. She also never attempted to call Lee's wife, Ellie Lou Cox. Bea considered herself much too classy a lady for that. Bea rationed that she had suffered the consequences of her actions and that was the chance she had taken. Somewhere inside herself, Bea had thought she deserved what she got from Lee, so she decided to bear the brunt of things and raise Bria by herself. Bea, being as proud as she was, did not let Lee know how much he had broken her heart or how deep her love for him truly was.

In 1960, when Bria was born, Earl and Bea doted over her like she was the first baby ever born. Eventually, Bea and Earl started attending the same local church Lee attended, and they would take Bria to church in the finest clothes any infant could wear. Bria was such a beautiful baby that by the end of day, Bea would often be one of the last to leave church as she tried to get the baby from whomever held Bria during Sunday service. Bea poured herself in the church even though the relationship with Lee had ended.

Lee was never fully out of Bea's life after Bria was born, and as time passed, Bea would allow Lee to visit and play with Bria.

Lee's visits continued even though Bea had started seeing other men. The new men were supposed to replace Lee, yet often did not fill the void. There was one relationship after the next. None seemed to satisfy Bea's cravings for Lee. It was like a woman wanting chocolate and eating sandwiches to suppress the desire. The more chocolate she craved, the more sandwiches she ate. Because the chocolate urge went unfulfilled, she ate more of what she didn't want. Lee was Bea's first love, but she knew she could not have him because Lee was a married man so Bea accepted the consequences of the hand she had been dealt.

Chapter Three

BEA DECIDED SHE WOULD START enjoying life.

She was still working at Bella's, but started to go to the nightclubs more. Late-night drinking and dancing became habitual for Bea who would go to the club so much that upon first approach at the bar to order a drink, the bartender, Trellis Scott, a tall, dark-complected and well-groomed man, would just set the Canadian Club on the rocks in a cocktail glass in front of her. Bea flirted with Trellis, and Trellis flirted with Bea. Trellis was about ten years older than Bea, the same as Lee. Trellis was married, too, but that didn't stop him from courting Bea.

Every evening, when Bea would end her shift at Bella's, she

would go to the Legion where Trellis was a bartender and sit at the end of the bar at what seemed like a seat reserved just for her.

Most folks during that time seemed to enjoy evenings at the Legion. It had become a favorite pastime for Bea and her associates. The night consisted of semi-professional cameramen taking black-and-white Kodak pictures where the ladies would be adorned with their finest dresses or two-piece skirt suits and the men wore suits. During those days, it wasn't uncommon for men to be dressed without a suitcoat, collared shirts, tie, and dress hats. Even the bartenders were uniformed in that time. They wore white shirts, black bowties, black dress pants and black satin aprons. Trellis, Bea's bartender, wore a black satin bowtie that crisscrossed and snapped at the neck. Trellis stepped up his attire from the ordinary apparel worn by the other bartenders by complementing his ensemble with a satin maroon-and-black brocade vest and nice black tuxedo trousers. Live entertainment was the thing then, which consisted of a three-man band, a singer, saxophonist, and pianist playing for the orderly and classy patrons of the evening.

Bea loved to dance and enjoyed showcasing her skills at the club as well as sitting at the bar keeping company with whatever girlfriend would happen to be out. Before Trellis and Bea became a couple, some of the men Bea met at the Legion would occasionally accompany her home. Often, Earl was already there while Bria would be in her bedroom sleeping. On the weekends, Earl preferred staying home to entertain friends versus the nightclubs, so he was the designated babysitter.

Earl didn't mind babysitting Bria. She was a quiet child who was content playing alone with her dolls and watching *The Jackie Gleason Show*. Typically afterward, Bria would go to bed and drift off to sleep. Earl had the house to himself during those evenings Bea went out. Earl knew just how to time things so his plans never collided with Bea's occasional rendezvous.

Bea started dating Trellis in 1966. After several months, Trellis' wife found out .

One Saturday evening as young Bria was sitting on a rug in their living room playing with her Barbie dolls in front of the television, she was distracted by a knock at the door. She went and tried to peek through the curtain covering the glass. She was dismayed to see an unfamiliar face there. The woman's knocking grew harder and more ferocious. The short, chubby woman started yelling and demanding Bria open the door. At first Bria couldn't make out her demands, then she heard her ask if Trellis was there. Bria, shaking by this time, shook her head no as the woman's tone got louder, and she yelled profanities. Bria was frozen, but was startled by the shattering glass bursting in the door. She stumbled backward.

"Help. Somebody help," Bria screamed.

"Oh my God. What is it? Bria, are you all right? What the hell is this? What happened?" Bea shouted as she ran from the bathroom to the front entrance, grabbing Bria's arm in a panic and looking at the shattered glass on the hardwood floor.

"I didn't do it, Bea. There was a lady at the door. First, she was knocking and asking if Trellis was here. I told her no, and she was yelling and cussing at me. She said...'stop lying, you little bitch,'" Bria said, sobbing. "Before I could go to try and find you and Uncle, she pulled out this big shiny thing and hit the glass and waved a gun at me. After she broke the glass, she ran to her car and took off."

"What? Waved a what?" Bea asked, startled.

By coincidence, Trellis wasn't at Bea's that night. Bea later told Trellis what had happened. This was it for Earl. He had already decided to move to the YMCA men's dorms and had grown tired of Bea's going out and binge drinking then coming home picking fights with him. This was the straw that broke the camel's back and also eventually led to Trellis asking his wife for a divorce.

Bea thought she had everything she wanted. She and Trellis barely waited for the ink to dry from his divorce before the two decided to get married.

Bea and Trellis had a few good years. Bea no longer worked for Bella's. She had gotten on at one of the local hardware plants. Bea earned a competitive salary, and for the first time had medical insurance benefits and profit sharing. During that time, a job with benefits was the reason most southern folk migrated to Illinois. After Trellis found a full-time job with the highway department of the state, he continued bartending part time on the weekends. Bea thought she and Trellis were doing pretty well for a while.

The marriage lasted approximately six years. About the third year, the fights started. Bria was around ten years old at the time when she would be awakened at night by cussing and shouting and things hitting the walls from Bea throwing stuff at Trellis. Bria once awoke to see Trellis with his left hand clasped around Bea's throat and the right hand balled in a tight fist and drawn back. Bria picked up a folding chair from her play dinette set to attempt to hit Trellis, which got Trellis' and Bea's attention.

"Bria, put the chair down, baby. I'm alright." Bea spoke in an even tone.

"Tell Trellis to stop before he hits you, Bea. Don't hurt my momma, Trellis, or I will hit you with this chair," Bria cried.

"Shiiit," Trellis said. "Hell, I'm not hurting her. I'm trying to keep her from knocking the hell out of me."

That evening ended with no one getting hurt. As the days went on, the fights would ensue again, and things would calm down as normal. The only difference was as time passed, Bria no longer jumped in the fights. She would simply close the door to her room and sit or lie on her bed and listen to the music from the small transistor radio she owned, trying to drown out the bickering and yelling outside her door. Music became Bria's escape from reality. Some of her favorite artists were the Fifth Dimension, Carole King, Tom Jones, and Three Dog Night. She knew all the lyrics and would sing along and pretend she was singing before a live audience. Bria had a vivid imagination as a child because she spent so much time alone, so she learned to entertain herself with the music to calm her nerves.

When there was peace in the house, Bria felt like she was walking on eggshells because at any given time, things could change. Later, Bria would overhear stories from her uncle Earl of how Bea started fights with Trellis at the bar. Uncle Earl said Bea would be so drunk sometimes that Trellis would secretly call him to come to the club to get her, so he would have to carry her out of the bar so Trellis could finish his job. Even though Uncle Earl took her home, Bea would manage to be up when

Trellis got there. Bria was told Bea would go into jealous rages and accuse Trellis of sleeping with the female waitresses as well as certain women patrons at the club.

As far back as Bria could remember, there seemed to be a fight between Bea and Trellis most weekends after the club. Bria hated hearing the bad stories about her mother and wondered why Uncle Earl told her such negative things when she never wanted to hear it.

In 1972, Bria was twelve. One day, out of the blue, Bea and Bria came home to find all of Trellis' belongings gone. Bea walked in their three-bedroom apartment as Bria followed and saw empty chest drawers that used to hold Trellis' clothes pulled out and some bare wire hangers slung on the bed where some of his white shirts and dress pants used to hang in the closets. Bria didn't know what to make of what she saw. Thinking back, Bria guessed six years was all Trellis could take of the marriage. Bea learned later Trellis had left for another woman.

As Bria recollected, that's when her life got real bad. Things started going downhill in the household—and fast. Bea withdrew from her close friends and family. She was no longer the pretty, well-dressed woman Bria admired. Bea let herself go. Because she worked the evening shift, Bea slept most of the day, which meant Bria was alone with no one to interact with. Bea continued to work her factory job, but had started drinking more and seeing more men.

Bria hated Bea's men friends. She was afraid of the men Bea dated and would retreat to her room when they came to the house. Bria wanted so badly to do something to hurt the men to keep them away from Bea, but she just didn't know what to do except feel sick and angry with Bea for allowing them at their home. They always came by in the evening. It was a different man but always after Bria's bedtime.

Bria was too young to know how to help her mother and did not know what their future would hold without Trellis around. What she felt in her heart was not good and was the turning point when her relationship with Bea changed. Bria longed for the old Bea back—the one when it was her, Bea, and Uncle Earl.

In Bria's mind, that's when she was happy and Bea was happy. Bria was pretty, she had nice pumps she would let Bria play in, but now Bea didn't have any of those things. Everything was a mess. Bria really missed the old days as mother and daughter between her and Bca. Bria didn't think Bea even realized what was happening and wondered if she even cared. Bea never asked Bria her feelings, so Bria never learned how to address what she liked or didn't like about her situation. The one time Bria tried to talk to Bea about how she felt, Bea yelled and cussed at her about being disrespectful and minding her own goddamn business, so Bria, not wanting to upset Bea, left things alone.

Although Bea was still attractive, the years of drinking had added weight, and working at the factory had aged her. Bea was no longer the classy dressing, sophisticated lady she was back in the early days working at working at Bella's. Bea had always been the kind of person who didn't care what others thought of her, so instead of her listening to the concerns of her brother, Earl, about how she as a single parent should be more focused on nurturing and caring for her child, Bea seemed to be oblivious to Earl's chastising. As far as Bea was concerned, Earl might as well have been talking to a wall. Bea was encapsulated by whatever it was that held her bound to that unformidable dark place, and no one, not even her precious baby girl, could bring her out of it. Bea's actions were rebellious and self-centered,

Bea had become wrapped up in her own issues. She did not take the time or effort to understand why she wasn't content with being alone, why she was making bad choices in men, or why she found comfort in drinking. Bea didn't deal with feelings or discuss hurt or disappointments. The only emotion she knew to display was anger.

Growing up with an alcoholic mother, Bria was familiar with not knowing what to expect from one day to the next. Their home environment was unpredictably unpredictable. Because of this chaos in their home, Bria didn't get many of her emotional needs met during those challenging times that would later impact her adult life.

In her adolescent years, Bria was forced to take on the maternal role. Bria cared for Bea as if she were the child. Bria helped her get to bed whenever she got too inebriated and had to sleep it off. Meanwhile, Bria found whatever she could to eat as she didn't want to disturb Bea. Bria was content with making a mayonnaise sandwich, or she would open a can of white hominy corn. Using a tad of butter, salt and pepper, she put all the ingredients in a saucepan, warmed it on the burner, poured it into a bowl and ate. Bread, milk, eggs, hominy corn and Argo brand white hard starch were the staples that Bea always had in the house. So Bria was confident she at least had something to eat and wouldn't go hungry.

Bea had also fallen off tidying up their apartment and was

not much of a housekeeper. Bria was embarrassed to have friends stop over after school. One reason was because she didn't know what condition Bea might be in; the other reason was Bria didn't want her friends to see how messy the house was. So Bria made it a point to greet her playmates at the door pretending she wasn't allowed to have company. Bria had perfected saying her goodbyes to her friends prior to reaching her front door so she could run ahead of them so her friends couldn't see the mess inside her home.

Bea's drinking escalated from the weekends to the weekdays, which led her to be hung over and too sick to get up for work. Bea missed work regularly. Some weeks she would miss a day then the next few weeks she would miss two days. Bria overheard Uncle Earl telling Bea to get it together, but Bea didn't care. She eventually lost her job of seven years because she missed three days of work without calling in. Over time, her new 1972 Buick Century got repossessed, and she and Bria were evicted from their rental home.

Bea and Bria had to live with relatives for a period of time until Bea could get back on her feet. Bria loved Bea even though she was ashamed of her behavior and longed for Bea to be different. Bria wanted so much for things to be normal again. Bria knew she didn't want to be like her mother and vowed she would never allow any men around her children unless she was married and in a committed relationship. Bria had also promised herself she would not become an alcoholic. Bria was always longing for a regular family life for herself. She was subconsciously always seeking something or someone to fill the void she longed for as it related to being regular. Bria always felt incomplete—not good enough—and even though Bria always received compliments from others who thought she was pretty, she was very insecure and shy.

Her caramel skin was flawless. Even through puberty, she never experienced pimples, acne, or any other adolescent skin issue. She had even white teeth, was medium size—not too thin and not too heavy—but had not been taught self-confidence nor had she ever been told by her mother that she was beautiful, so she never felt such.

All Bria knew was that she felt neglected and alone. Sometimes she fantasized about being adopted and what that would feel like. Bria wanted a family with a mother and father. There was no father in her house except for the period Bea and Trellis were married, but Trellis wasn't much of a father to Bria. Trellis didn't abuse or mistreat her. He just never went out of his way to establish a relationship with her. The only father she knew was Uncle Earl. As much as she loved Uncle Earl, he just wasn't enough to fill the father void she was missing. Uncle Earl was good to her—always there when she needed him—and she knew Uncle Earl loved her and that he was proud of her, but still he could not fill that empty space.

For a short time, Bea was involved with a man named Theodis Rickman. Bria was too young to remember Lee, her biological father, so over the years, Bea had said Theodis was Bria's father. Bria never knew for sure when Theodis showed up because there had been so many men coming and going for a while that she couldn't keep up. She did remember Theodis was one of the nicer guys, and as she grew older, Theodis would come around once a week to drop off twenty dollars to Bea, saying it was for child support, and on occasion he would give Bria an extra five dollars. To Bria, that was as good as it got to having a daddy outside of Uncle Earl, but she rarely saw Uncle Earl anymore because he chose not to come around much due to Bea's constant drinking.

On one of Theodis' visits, Bria jokingly asked Theodis why he didn't come by more often and spend any time with her. Theodis had said he didn't come around much because Bea was so difficult to deal with, and she would give him a hard time by always cussing, fussing, and starting chaos. Bria accepted that and didn't really fault Theodis because she knew firsthand how Bea could be. In spite of Theodis' reasoning, Bria never really felt any connection to Theodis. She was fond of Theodis. He seemed to be a good man. He didn't cuss or drink. He had a hearty laugh and seemed mild tempered, but Bria just never felt a sense of connection with him. She didn't know why she felt that way, but Theodis did not feel like he was her real daddy no matter how he acted. It was as if something real was missing. As easygoing as he was, Bria often wondered how Theodis dealt with Bea in the first place because their personalities were so opposite.

Going forward, Bria decided not to question Theodis and Bea's relationship because she had grown content and was satisfied for the time being. As it turned out, Theodis seemed to like pretending he was her father and represented her well. As far as she was concerned, he was her father. Bria thought it felt good fitting in with the rest of her friends who all came from two-parent households. She didn't know what really went on in her friends' homes. All she knew was what she saw on the outside, but to let Bea tell it, so-and-so cheated on his wife all the time, and Mrs. So-and-so had a boyfriend she kept when Mr. So-and-so was at work. One of Bea's favorite sayings was "So-and-so think they hot shit walking on a stick, but they ain't shit... They always tryna keep up with the Joneses." Bria rarely believed her and didn't know why Bea made up such stories about other people.

As hard as times were, Bea still managed to send Bria to one of the best Catholic schools in the local area. While Bea liked to do her own thing—drinking, sleeping around with married men, and partying—she tried to keep a watchful eye on Bria and had instilled some morals and values in Bria similar to what she learned from her own religious mother. For Bea, it was "do as I say not as I do," so she taught and reinforced etiquette and poise. Bria was to say *please* and *thank you.* Bea emphasized how to be a lady—be a good girl, don't lie, go to church on Sundays—some of which contradicted how she lived, but she taught Bria otherwise. These were the things Bea held pride in.

Bria felt like an only child because she was not raised in Alabama with her siblings. Things were good with Bria and Bea for about the first twelve years of Bria's life. As a young girl Bria had numerous items like Barbie dolls, a new bicycle, books, clothes, and stuffed animals to hold her attention as Bea compensated Bria with material things for the lack of attention she provided due to devoting time to her relationships with men and other life circumstances.

So coming up Bria was exposed to expensive clothes, shoes, her favorite Barbie dolls, her own television—things her friends thought were luxuries, she had. In the early days, Bria remembered how Bea played the Santa Claus role at Christmastime, how she played the tooth fairy role when a tooth fell out, how she even left baskets filled with candy and eggs from the so-called Easter Bunny during Easter, and almost never missed giving Bria a party and gifts for birthdays. Bria loved the fantasy world Bea had created for her, but as soon as Bria got older, that life changed, and reality set in.

Bria noticed a difference after Trellis left. Bea became reclusive, days upon days not getting out of bed, sleeping off and on, and keeping to herself, which led to Bea disengaging the both of them from family gatherings. Bria would try to be as quiet as possible around their home, not wanting to disturb Bea since she knew it was better to leave Bea alone than for her to be bothered. Otherwise, she ran the risk of Bea being abrasive and drinking alcohol, neither of which Bria wanted to endure. Bria learned to entertain herself alone. Bria's favorite pastimes became reading the Nancy Drew series books, comics in the daily newspaper, and listening to songs on the radio. It was peaceful, and Bria allowed her imagination to take her to places away from the present. She dreamed that one day she would be happy and live a life surrounded by beautiful things, people who loved her and a home filled with joy and laughter.

Chapter Four

THIS WAS A HARD LESSON that didn't just come overnight. Bria was fifteen when she got pregnant with her first child, a son, Zachary Twon. She was young, insecure, and very naïve. She had been caught up with trying to fit in with other popular girls. She had fallen head over heels—or so she thought—in love with Zach's father, Leon Reynolds. He was her next-door neighbor and a classmate, her first real boyfriend and the very first male she had been attracted to, and the feeling was mutual.

Bria knew Bea had not ever talked about the facts of life with her, except for the time when Bria started her menstrual cycle. Bria had been so afraid when she started that she took a washcloth, folded it, and put it in her underwear to catch the bleeding because she didn't have any sanitary napkins. But Bea eventually found the bloody towels and confronted Bria about it. By her actions, the first thing Bea assumed was Bria had been raped. She didn't say it, but the look she had on her face said it all. Bria could tell Bea was relieved when she said no. Bea soon after realized what it was, bought Bria Kotex, and that was it. There were no further discussions about it.

Bria hadn't been exposed to anyone telling her that young men sometimes give young girls flattering compliments only to lead to something more compromising. Leon told her things that made her feel good, and she believed him.

Bria was naïve and thought she was too smart to become pregnant, even though she knew what she and Leon had been doing was wrong, risky, and irresponsible. Becoming a teenage mother was the farthest thing from her mind. All she knew was Leon said he liked her and she liked him—he was her boyfriend, she was his girlfriend, and finally she had someone she thought she could trust. She thought if she did not allow him certain pleasures, then he wouldn't like her and she wouldn't have anyone. She was devastated when their relationship changed after giving birth to Zach. Bria was hurt and thought it was a slap in the face when Leon even had the nerve to say Zach wasn't his child.

Bria wished she had listened to Bea who had been trying to prevent what ultimately happened. Bea kept saying, stuff like, "I can't stand that li'l black ass boy. He's up to no good. That boy is coming over here too much. That boy needs to go home," but Bria wouldn't listen. She would not believe Leon would betray her the way he did. She had been a straight-A student all throughout her freshman year. During the pregnancy, Bria knew she had let down Bea; so many other people including, Uncle Earl; several teachers; not to mention some of her close relatives and friends. So Bria was determined to make the best of a bad situation to prove to herself and them she was not a failure.

After pressure by some of their kinfolk to give Zach up for adoption, Bria refused and was determined to continue regular school. She would not drop out. She made up her mind she was not going to attend night school as her school counselor recommended. She pushed herself and managed to only miss the first two weeks of her sophomore year so she could continue school and graduate with her class as originally planned. She told herself she would live up to the promise she made to herself and her unborn children that she would by any means necessary be a good mother and provide her children with everything and more than she ever had in her life

Leon didn't see things the way Bria did. Leon, being only sixteen at the time, still in high school and unemployed was embarrassed and ashamed as well. To protect his innocence in the situation, he denied being Zach's father and spread rumors that Bria was sleeping with other young men at their school. He even told his parents this story.

It wasn't until a blood test was ordered by the Public Assistance Department to which she was forced to apply that Leon finally admitted to his responsibility. By then, Bria had so much disdain and animosity toward him that she vowed Leon would not ever have to worry about helping with her child. Zach was her child and that was all that mattered. At that time, Bria never once thought to ask Leon how he was feeling or what he might have been going through. She didn't care. She only cared about Zach and what she needed to do to provide for him.

Life got busy fast after Zach was born. Bria went to school in the day and immediately found a job at the public library in the evenings. During her quiet moments, she often reflected on the past and how it impacted her present. Bria felt she had grown up pretty fast. It was like after she acknowledged to Bea she no longer believed in Santa Claus, her reality literally changed.

As a child, Bria had felt smart when she approached Bea one season and said, "I know there's no Santa. It's you who's putting all those gifts out." That moment changed Bria's life forever. It was then that her mother cut out the fantasy and fairy tale of buying gifts she couldn't afford, going through the effort of displaying the gifts under a tree during the night while Bria slept, eating Christmas cookies and pretending Santa ate them. From that point on, Bria had to deal with life on more realistic terms.

As young as Bria was, it seemed from the age of fifteen she had been in one relationship after the next. She never gave herself time to breathe. Almost immediately after the relationship with Leon had gone bad, Bria met and dated a guy named Omar Williams. Omar had approached Bria while she was at a grocery store with a friend during her pregnancy with Zach. Omar's boldness impressed her as she recalled the meeting with one of her high school friends, Juanita Hill.

"Girl, you know yesterday after school that guy Omar Williams that we saw at the Piggly Wiggly the other day approached me and complimented my appearance, then he asked for my phone number. Can you believe that? What kind of a guy looks at a pregnant chick? Not only that, how is he asking for my number and I'm pregnant? What kind of stuff is that?" Bria asked, talking on the phone to Juanita one school evening.

"Why do you act so surprised, Bria? You know Omar is always looking at you at school. You won't be pregnant forever girl, damn," Juanita said.

"Yeah, but you have to wonder what's wrong with a dude for asking a pregnant girl for her phone number. Maybe he's hard up or something," Bria said.

"Bowlegged as that boy is, he don't look hard up to me. Girl, stop tripping. You're smart and gorgeous. The boy ain't blind. He can see that. So what you made a mistake and got pregnant. As bad as it is, it ain't the end of the world. Maybe Omar sees you for who you are and not for what—or shall I say who—is in your womb. Give him a chance," Juanita said.

Weeks passed, and Bria hadn't seen Omar since their initial meeting at the Piggly Wiggly store. Bria was a sophomore and he was a junior in high school. Bria gave birth to Zach in August 1976, the summer before her sophomore year. Prior to the start of school, Bria and Bea had already made arrangements for a babysitter for Zach, so on the third week Bria was set to go. She arrived at school with Mesha Jones, one of her classmates.

"The bell's ringing. I'll see you after class. Meet me in Black Corner," Bria said as she slammed the orange hall locker.

"Alright, girl. For a second there, I had to think what Black Corner was, but I forgot that's what we call the spot where we all congregate in between classes. You know I'm slow, girl. I'm glad you're back. See you after class," Mesha responded.

Bria walked into the oblong room and chose a seat at one the wooden tables strategically located in lecture style inside the classroom. As all the students began to fill the space, Bria literally almost wet her pants when Omar walked in. Bria acted like she didn't see him entering and kept her head straight, focused on the blackboard at the front.

Don't tell me he's in my art class, Bria thought.

Weeks went by before Omar finally made his move and asked Bria for her phone number again. The two started talking. Omar's next move was offering to give Bria a ride home from school. One day turned into every day. Bria and Omar seemed like they were two of the high school's perfect couples. Bria was happy again to have someone as her own and to have a steady companion to go to the Friday night basketball and football games. It made her feel good that Omar showed her so much attention in public. Omar introduced Bria to all his friends. Bria met Omar's parents before he eventually informed his mother that Bria had a child.

"Bria, why don't you ever bring your little boy when you come here?" Mrs. Williams, Omar's mother, asked.

Looking somewhat surprised and ashamed, Bria didn't know what to say, which was reflected by her expression.

"Baby, it's okay. Omar told me you have a baby. Bring him by so we can meet him. There's no way I can judge anyone for anything. I had Omar when I was a teenager, so I know how it is. You bring that baby to me so I can love on him," Mrs. Williams said.

Bria was relieved by Mrs. Williams' comment and was glad to know she no longer had to hide her baby and pretend he didn't exist when she visited their home. So the next time, Bria brought Zach along. She saw firsthand how much Mrs. Williams welcomed her and Baby Zach into their home.

Bria loved being in the Williamses' home. Mrs. Williams was very religious and involved in church. She loved to bake cakes and was a very good cook. Often when Bria and Omar would come in, Mrs. Williams would be preparing one of her favorites, either a German chocolate three-layered cake or 7-Up pound cake for some church function. The Williamses seemed to have the type of family life Bria envisioned for her own life. Bria loved being around the family and loved being included. During the holidays, when not much was going on around Bea's house, which was often, Bria would welcome and accept the invitations from the Williamses to celebrate in their home. They would have large family gatherings and lots and lots of homemade food—fried chicken, cornbread dressing, macaroni and cheese, spaghetti, potato salad, turnip greens, candied sweet potatoes, and baked cakes—for days as folks would say.

Unknown to Bria then, and true to what Bea had always said, nobody's family was perfect, and everyone had issues to deal with. This statement rang true when Bria discovered Omar was struggling in school and had fallen so academically far behind that he was on the verge of not graduating. She couldn't understand how. As close as they had gotten, he hadn't shared that piece of information with her.

Before Bria had a chance to discuss the issue with Omar, he had already decided to quit school because he felt it was too hard to make up his graduation credits. Omar's stepfather and mother tried to dissuade him, but he insisted on doing what he wanted to do. After seeing there was no changing his mind,

Omar's stepdad got him a job at the local steel foundry. Omar convinced Bria it was the best alternative for not only him, but it was an opportunity for him to provide a good life for her and Zach because of the good pay from the job.

Omar told Bria he planned to work hard and save so they could get married. Bria bought into the idea and hoped it would complete her own fantasy of a dream family and normalcy. Being young and still in school, Bria found she still longed to do the things that teenagers her age typically did, but with Zach she discovered some limitations due to not having someone to babysit. Since Omar had quit school, he had to work, leaving Bria alone. Growing tired of the adultlike routine and her complaints, Omar began to skip most Friday night shifts to be at the football games with Bria and their other schoolmates. Omar soon became controlling and jealous of Bria, which led to him skipping shifts and ultimately losing his job. Bria soon realized she could no longer tolerate Omar's behavior and decided to break up with him.

As Bria went about the course of trying to complete life without Omar, he became obsessed with trying to get her back. Bria would tell her girlfriends that Omar was her fatal attraction. During the breakup period, he would show up at any given time, no matter who she was with or where they were, begging and pleading for her to take him back. This went on for several months. It got to the point that Bria had to have someone with her at all times until Bea arrived home from work. The relationship with Omar turned into one of life's experiences that helped to shape her character—the past helping to shape the future. Bria learned at a young age what not to look for in a man.

Omar was compassionate and kind in the beginning, but he turned out to be an insecure, compulsive liar. The relationship lasted a year or so, and it didn't end easily. He didn't give up without a fight. He continued to come around and harass her for many months.

What put an end to his surprise visits was an alcohol-empowered Bea who threatened to whip his ass with the handle of a butcher knife. Bria could never figure out how Bea didn't cut her own hand the way she held onto that knife—must have been a dull blade was what she thought. Omar must have believed Bea was crazy enough to harm him because he didn't show his face around their small house again after that incident. This was even after numerous episodes of Omar coming to their home uninvited. Bria thought it was peculiar that Omar wasn't afraid of the restraining order or the numerous times she had threatened to call the police for his uninvited pop-up visits, but when it came to the fear of Bea, that seemed to be all it took.

The next boyfriend in Bria's steady stream of men was named Stetson Miller. He was about five years her senior. Bria was glad things had calmed with the Omar ordeal and assumed he finally got the message it was over between them.

Bria met Stetson during the summer of 1978. Bria was hanging out with some friends at a park on the southwest side of Rockford known as the popular spot for African-American youth. The temperature was in the eighties, the park was crowded with high schoolers who ranged from freshmen through graduating seniors along with some of the first-year college students who were home for break.

Bria always enjoyed the atmosphere there as she watched

guys on the basketball court, girls sitting on swings as they talked and flirted back and forth with the group. Bria was joined by Juanita and another one of her girlfriends, Meshalette Jones whom they called Mesha. Juanita was tall and model-like, fair skinned and very made up. Juanita seemed to meet no strangers, and she mostly got along with everyone.

Mesha, on the other hand, was very outgoing, an attractive dark-skinned, slender, bow-legged young lady with a protruding butt. Mesha loved going to the park as well because she generally received a lot of attention from the young men. Usually, when it was the three of them, it was Mesha, Juanita, then Bria in that order. Mesha always got the popular, fine guys. Bria seemed to get the leftovers.

It was the summer of 1978. This particular time at the park, Bria was sitting in her car, a small used 1970 orange and black vinyl top Pontiac Firebird, listening to music with Zach in the backseat. Mesha and Juanita were each having individual conversations with Edmond and Joshua Stewart who were nicknamed E and Ja and considered two of the finest brothers at Rockford High. Bria heard a voice that said, "Damn, introduce me to your friend, man."

"No, problem, my man," E replied and grabbed Juanita by the arm.

"Juanita, this is Stetson Miller. We call him Stet. He's my main man, closer than a brother," E said.

"Nice to meet you, Stetson," Juanita said.

Bria looked at what was going on from the side mirror of the car.

"Man, you're my brother, and Juanita's friend in the car here is like a sister. I think she is the perfect person for you. I can talk to this lady about anything. I trust her second next to my mother. Bria girl, get out that car. You have to meet my brother," E said.

Bria was slightly embarrassed by E's bold behavior and comments and thought, *No, he didn't* as she got out the car and pretended not to notice Stetson who was dressed in athletic shorts, a white t-shirt, and Puma gym shoes, and was straddled on an expensive ten-speed bike as he looked at her from the moment she got out of the car to the point of their eye contact.

Bria extended her hand and said, "How are you? Nice to meet you."

"Oh, I'm cool. How are you? You from around here?" Stetson asked.

"I'm fine, and yes I'm from around here—born and raised," Bria said.

"Yeah, you are...fine that is. Who is the little man in the backseat?" Stetson asked.

"Oh, this is my son, Zach. Say what's up to Stetson," Bria said.

"Vrrrroom, vrrroom," Zach responded.

"What's up, little man?" Stetson said.

Zach seemed to care less about the introduction as he was preoccupied with a toy car, running it over the car seat.

"You have a number or sumthin' I can reach you at, that is if you don't mind me calling you sometime? I don't mean to be so forward, but E will tell you, I'm sort of a no-nonsense, straight-to-the-point type of guy, so you mind if I get your number?" Stetson asked Bria.

"Sure. I guess that would be cool," Bria said. She leaned back over into the car and picked up a pen and a note pad from her purse, then jotted down her phone number.

"How about I give you a call tomorrow? What's a good time for you?" Stetson asked.

"Well, if all goes as planned, I'll be starting at Rock Valley College. I'm hoping to get morning classes so any time after noon should work. On second thought, I work one to five, so any time after say six would be better," Bria said.

"Cool. I'll check you out around six-thirty, maybe even seven—give you time to get little man settled," Stetson said.

"Cool," Bria said and watched as Stetson slapped five to E and Ja before he took off.

"Be cool, bro. Gotta run." He looked at Bria. "I'll talk to you tomorrow."

As planned, Bria had completed high school and was looking forward to the first day of pursuing higher education at the community college. She looked at it as a chance to create a better life for her and Zach so she could fulfill a promise to herself to not have him grow up the way she had.

At first Bria hadn't given much thought to meeting Stetson because since the breakup with Omar she had become so used to her friends' attempt to introduce her to guys who after they found out she had a child didn't call her. So that day at the college it caught her off guard when she ran into Stetson in the student center.

"Hey. What's up, girl? You look like you done seen a ghost," Stetson said.

"Hey...I'm surprised to see you here," Bria said.

"Yeah. I have a couple classes I'm finishing up before I get my associate's degree. I'm glad I ran into you though. Where are you headed?" Stetson asked.

"Oh, I didn't know you were a student here. You didn't mention that when we met," Bria said.

"Well, we haven't talked since the day we met, so how could you know? In other words, we haven't had time to get that acquainted yet. Like I asked, where are you headed? Or better yet what time is your last class? Maybe we can grab a quick somethin' to eat before you head off... If I recall, you said you work after school. Am I right?" Stetson said.

Bria thought things with Stetson would be different since he was five years older than she was. She was impressed with him and was intrigued even more that he was in college. Over the course of days as they spent more time together, they got to know each other better. Days turned into weeks, and weeks turned into months as Bria noticed Stetson hadn't asked her to be his lady yet, so she was somewhat unsure of what to expect out of the relationship.

Between Omar and Stetson, Bria had sporadically dated a couple guys who had taken her out, but who seemed to be interested in one thing—going to bed with her—and she had eventually found out they weren't just sleeping with her but a few others. As she thought about those past guys and experiences, it wasn't something she was proud of, and she often tried to block it from her memory.

Secretly, Bria knew she had been somewhat promiscuous out of insecurity and to prove her value. All she had to go on was what she saw growing up with Bea, so she tolerated how she was treated by the guys she dealt with and believed it was what she deserved. Bria and Stetson had been a year into their relationship and had not discussed feelings or what either wanted or expected from each other. So as far as she was concerned, she and Stetson were not exclusive to each other in terms of being in a committed relationship. Stetson called it having an open relationship, which meant he was seeing other women. As far as Bria was concerned, and since Stetson did not want to be committed, she saw other men as well.

She thought differently after one incident that caused an unexpected confrontation with Stetson. One evening while she was visiting Stetson at his apartment, he informed her he had been burned. Not knowing what that meant, she was stunned at his tone and soon figured out he had contracted a sexually transmitted disease. Bria was speechless and thought her face was literally about to fall off. Stetson comforted her and continued to talk her through what had occurred and educated her on what she needed to do medically to have herself checked out. He then preceded to tell her it was time they cut out the game playing and became serious about each other. At that moment, Bria agreed, although she never confided she had been promiscuous, and as far as she knew, contracting the infection could have been just as much her fault as it had been his.

Bria regretted she and Stetson had to go through those past indiscretions to get to a point of having a one-on-one relationship. But she was relieved to have the past behind them so they could move forward. To Bria, the way Stetson handled that situation further confirmed to her his maturity level. Their relationship grew stronger over time. They became a couple and met each other's folks. Bria admired the closeness within his family and how they accepted Zach and welcomed him.

A couple years into the relationship, in 1981, Bria got pregnant with a second child, a daughter whom they decided to name India. Stetson was proud of his baby girl but still had not asked Bria to marry him. Bria realized she needed more income for Zach and India, so she decided to quit school and work full time. Bria realized she had lost her consistency in school. Had she been more focused on her education, she would have been done with school. Instead she lacked the required hours to get her associate's degree, all due to dropping classes and other distractions along the way. Although Stetson was a good provider, she felt she needed to be more independent than to rely on a man to take care of Zach, India, as well as herself she refused to raise her kids on welfare.

By about 1984, Bria's life started to transform for the better. This was when she got her first well-paying job with the Con Ed Electric Company. She was so elated when she received the call of being offered the position and left her life was finally beginning. Her new position was with the nuclear plant a division of the electric company as an entry-level clerk. She was excited to get medical benefits, vacation, 401(k), and tuition reimbursement, and was also provided opportunities to advance within the company. Bria felt accomplished and that things were looking up for her and the kids even without a husband.

She was twenty-four and had two children, Zach and India. Bria figured she wanted more out of life because she had so many bad childhood memories. She recalled hearing someone say you should be careful of envying others because you never know what that person had to go through in life to get to where they are. She knew firsthand what that meant. She often wondered why she had to go through all the pain, shame, and embarrassment she did as a child. Looking back over her life, she realized her past helped shape her into the person she was now, and she tried to convince herself she wouldn't have had it any other way. But Bria wasn't sure that was the case, which was one reason why she had made sure her children would know, no matter how good or bad, who their biological fathers were so they wouldn't have to grow up wondering. She wanted them to know who they were and where they came from.

Bria read somewhere that psychological studies show that children raised without fathers can lead to kids having issues such as aggressiveness, depression, low self-esteem, doing poorly in school, doing drugs, and other deviant behavior. Bria knew firsthand being raised without her own father, she had developed an inferiority complex and lacked self-esteem, and she always longed for validation and affirmation from others. She spent a good majority of her life struggling with thoughts of wanting to be like other people and wishing her mom was more supportive. Her naiveté led her to believe if she had a father, life would have been better. So if possible she would see to it that her children didn't go through the same scenario.

Bria vowed to herself not to make the same mistake as Bea. She tried not to talk bad about Zach's father and wanted him to develop a relationship of his own with his dad. As hard as it was, she wanted him to form his own opinions, regardless of whether things hadn't worked out between her and the past relationship. She had grown to understand that growing up without a father had caused some hardship in her life and wanted to shield Zach from that melodrama. Meanwhile, she planned to do all she could to see to it that her son did not have to deal with any similar feelings of inadequacies. Bria wanted what was best for her son, and if that meant she had to co-parent, then that's what she intended to do. Her issue was sometimes his father didn't reciprocate, and she was left trying to provide a stable and healthy environment for Zach all alone.

Bria always knew she was somewhat a dreamer. That was how she had learned to cope with things as she grew up. When it came time to be a parent, she knew what *not* to do. Bria thought she had it all worked out, surmising it would be left up to the fathers to make or break their relationship with their children. Having gone through her life experiences, she would not want any child of hers to bear the same burden. She made these mental promises to herself and secretly vowed to keep them. Among the list, she vowed never to bad mouth either of her children's fathers in front of them.

Bria had been with Stetson while she was still living with Bea. She knew not to bring another child home, so she soon found an apartment, thinking she, Stetson, Zach and India would all be together. Bea would tell Bria all the time just because she had Zach and India didn't make her a mother. Some of her exact words were, "You act like you're the only one done had children. Well, you're not. You don't know nuthin' 'bout being a mother 'cause you ain't been through enough yet. Just keep living, you'll see. And don't even think that man gon' care about what you and them kids are going through 'cause he don't give one flyin' damn. Believe what I'm tellin' you 'cause I done been through it. I know what I'm talkin' 'bout. You gon' have to get out there and get it for you and them kids yourself."

Bea's words stung Bria like a bee. She wouldn't ever forget what Bea said. Bria realized her mother didn't always use tact, but she had a way of saying things that cut to the chase, and she wouldn't back down from how she said them. There had been something else Bea had always warned Bria about, which Bria overlooked or pretended not to know: Stetson was a well-known drug dealer.

Bria had heard the stories from others over time, but since she had no firsthand evidence, she acted like she didn't know. But what she had noticed was since he'd finished school, he never worked other than deejaying at parties over the weekends. When she would bring it up, he would dismiss it and tell her not to worry about it, and it was better for her not ask certain questions. Bria was okay with things the way they were. She had provided a nice home for her kids, her job, and some help from Stetson when she needed it, so she was content—or so she thought.

As time went on, Bria noticed a change in Stetson's behavior which led to a strained dynamic in their relationship. For one, Bria thought it was odd that he was out until the wee hours of the morning outside of the typical timeframe Friday through Sunday since most of Stetson's gigs were held over the weekend at after sets, which were generally held at someone's house or basement depending on the host of the party and were held after a bar lounge closed at 1 A.M. So Bria expected to see him around four or five in the morning give or take considering the time it took to take down his equipment.

Stetson had always been what some would call an alpha male. Bria had been intrigued by him because he was confident, the leader of his crew, the one others looked up to, and always in control. To some outsiders, he appeared somewhat arrogant, but as of late, when he showed up at her place, he had mood swings, displayed paranoia, he acted jittery and anxious for no apparent reason along with making unjust infidelity accusations against Bria when such was not the case. To make matters worse Bria couldn't tolerate his tone of voice when he spoke to her, she couldn't exactly pinpoint the change in Stetson, but over time she made a mental note that things could no longer proceed as they were.

Bria tried to overlook Stetson's actions because she didn't want to lose the relationship and believed there was too much time invested. Most weekends the kids spent time with Bea or their play godfamily who in actuality had been the neighbors to Bea and Bria over the years. But they loved Bria and the kids and would help out whenever possible because the mother of the family knew Bria had been a young mother.

So Bria took advantage of the free time from the kids and spent the time going out with her friends, then later meeting up with Stetson at whatever venue he spun records at. Bria thought things would be better if she hung out with him more, so she eventually started going to the after sets with Stetson. At first, Bria enjoyed dressing up and getting made up to go out to the parties. It all seemed like fun for a while until the party was over. It was afterward when he and his buddies would pull out the cocaine and free-base paraphernalia. Bria found herself doing cocaine with him and his friends and their girlfriends to try and fit it, but to her dismay, she started to enjoy the high.

For a while Bria's drug of choice was tooting coke. She never indulged in smoking weed, reefer as it was called back then, but she did indulge in the coke, which later progressed to her decision to try free basing. The euphoria was so different, but it lasted momentarily, so she had to pull from the pipe frequently to maintain that same sense of high.

It got to the point she and Stetson started getting high at her apartment after the kids were put to bed. It got so regular that she wondered how she managed to go to work afterward. The final straw was an encounter where she had gotten so high that she thought she was losing her breath. She grabbed her chest and went and laid on the floor of her children's room. All she could visualize was Zach waking up and finding her dead. She cried and pleaded, "God, please help me" and promised if the Lord would save her life she would not do drugs ever again.

It took some time before Bria realized she needed to make a change. That one experience woke her up, but it was still not enough for her to see the light. She stopped free basing, but she would occasionally toot the white powder with Stetson and a couple of friends. Their relationship had gone on for six years. Bria had begun to feel Stetson had taken her for granted. He was abrupt when he spoke to her in public, and more and more, she felt disrespected.

Mentally, Bria began to strategize how to get out of the relationship as she had come to the conclusion this was not the lifestyle she wanted for her kids. In her mind, Bria was reminded of Theodis and Bea's bad relationship and how that made her feel as a child, so she knew she wanted someone who would better match her vision of a healthy family and someone with a less risky lifestyle. She made up her mind she could no longer wait for Stetson to change. At that point, she didn't think he ever would, but she knew it was time to end their relationship.

Not long after Bria broke up with Stetson, she made her next move, and like Tarzan of the jungle, she swung into the next guy named Radcliffe Smith whom she called Rad. Since that relationship with Stetson, Bria had sworn off men for a while or so she thought, but then that was before being introduced to Rad.

Bria and Rad met in 1987 through a mutual friend, Dale Cummings. Bria had known Dale and his wife, Lynette, for several years before being introduced to Rad. Dale and Lynette had arranged an evening of fun and entertainment at a local spot called Main & Island on the south side of Rockford. Dale had previously talked Rad into meeting Bria on a blind date of which Lynette had coordinated by encouraging Bria to come. At first, Bria wasn't attracted to him because of his age. Lynette and Dale told her Dale was ten years older, but that he was a fun guy who knew how to have a good time. This piqued Bria's interest, and she agreed to meet Dale anyhow despite her previous reservations.

"Girl, I am not into blind dates. You sure this guy isn't some psycho nut?" Bria asked.

"Girl, ain't nobody asking you to marry the man. Just meet him. You might have fun," Lynette responded.

"Yeah, I suppose. Well, we'll be in a public place, so it should be alright, right?"

"Dang, Bria. I thought you were more outgoing and uninhibited than that. What happened? Shit, you taught me a thing or two in my day," Lynette said.

"Yeah, but back then AIDS and shit wasn't running rampant in the land. You have to be careful these days. Folks on crack. Shiiiit, things ain't like it used to be," Bria said.

"You sure are right, but I think this guy will be alright. You know I wouldn't let Dale hook you up with just anybody. Besides, if he's not, we're in a club setting, so you're free to dance with whomever you like, no strings attached," Lynette said.

After the two met, Bria and Rad danced and talked all evening. Through their casual conversation, Bria learned Rad's mother was a single parent too, and he was the oldest of his brothers and sisters. She liked his personality and was fond of his tales regarding his somewhat rambunctious mother. Bria began to feel a sense of commonality and connection with Rad and believed she had met someone who would accept her for who she was, and she was glad they had come from similar backgrounds.

Bria shared she was the youngest of four but raised as an only child because her mother Bea had left the other children in Alabama with her parents. Rad and Bria seemed to connect instantly. At least in Bria's mind they connected. Bria always had a problem relating to most men or any individual for that matter who seemed to be more than what Bria thought she was. Bria would later learn that insecurity drove her to settle for things in relationships that were not always positive.

Rad seemed to be just the type of guy Bria had longed for. He was tall, handsome, well versed, dressed nicely, liked to dance and had a sense of humor. Bria was on her third Tanqueray and tonic drink for the night when the bartender announced last call for alcohol.

"Are you driving? I can give you a ride home," Rad said, turning up his shot of Hennessey.

"Well, Lynette, I suppose I could let you and Dale go on. I'll talk to you tomorrow," Bria responded.

"Sure. Go ahead dump us. That's alright. Just joking, girl. Go ahead. I have his license plate number, his address, and his momma's name. He won't try anything," Lynette joked.

"Lynette, you know you're crazy. My man Rad is cool. Bria couldn't be in better hands. Looks like a love connection," Dale said to Rad.

"Okay, man. I got your love connection," Rad said.

"I'll check you later, dude," Dale said.

He put his empty shot glass on the bar and gentlemanly extended his hand to escort her from her chair.

Bria slipped out of the seat and walked ahead, leaving the main lounge.

Rad was watching the reflection of Bria's curvaceous hips on the mirror-lined walls while exiting the lounge.

"You know you're a pretty good dancer," Rad said to Bria while opening the car door to his Fleetwood Cadillac.

"You aren't so bad yourself," Bria responded.

"Where to, my lady? The night is still young. What time is curfew?" Rad asked.

"*Hmmm,* let's see. It's after twelve, and I haven't turned into a pumpkin, so I guess I'm good to go. What did you have in mind?" Bria asked, knowing the kids were with a sitter.

"Let's just drive and see where we end up," Rad said.

"You know what? On second thought, why don't you come

over to my place and I'll make us some breakfast. I make a delicious Denver omelet," she suggested.

"Bria's kitchen. Omelets it is then. Show me the way," Rad responded.

Bria gave Rad directions to her house. The night still seemed as hot and humid as it had been earlier in the day. The only breeze came from the movement in the car. Rad had insisted, and Bria didn't object to riding with the windows down versus using the air conditioning.

When they arrived at the house, there was no omelet making, only lovemaking, and the rest would lead to the beginning of another relationship.

Weeks passed, and Bria and Rad had seen each other at least twice a week. Bria slowly introduced Rad to Zach and India. The four would go to the movies, the park and sometimes would have the occasional home-cooked soul food dinner—beans, cornbread, macaroni and cheese, roast surrounded by potatoes, carrots and onions and the usual sweet tea, all prepared by Bria.

Chapter Five

ZACH WAS NOW TWELVE YEARS OLD and very protective of his mom. He was not overly thrilled by the whole relationship thing with Rad being there, and especially not content with sharing his mother's attention with another man. As time went on, he began to show signs of his disapproval. Bria seemed oblivious to her son's discontentment.

So much so several weeks had passed, and Bria and Rad continued to spend endless evenings together. Bria was constantly coming up with creative ideas to entice Rad. On one particular Friday night after work, Bria had asked Rad to come by for an intimate dinner for just the two of them. Zach and India were spending the weekend with Bea, so Bria decided to prepare a meal that would consist of a salad, stuffed pasta shells, and garlic bread. The pasta dish was a recipe she got from one of her friends and was told it was easy but looked elegant enough it would win any man's heart. Bria went all the way. She played soft music, lit candles and set the table to her four-chair glass dinette table with porcelain plates, linen, and wineglasses.

"Damn that was a very good meal. I think I'm out of my league," Rad said.

"Why would you say that, Rad? This was just a simple meal, real simple—pasta, spaghetti sauce, meat, some shells and a salad. What's the big deal?"

"Yeah, whatever. Well, no one has ever gone to this type of trouble to impress me like this before. Hey, there's something I've been meaning to talk to you about," Rad said.

"Really...well, whatever you say. So what is it you want to talk to me about?" Bria asked.

"I don't think Zach cares too much for his momma having a man around, Bria," Rad said.

"So what makes you think this? I don't think it bothers Zach at all that you and I are seeing each other," Bria said.

"I don't think you've been paying attention. Just check him out sometimes. You'll see what I mean."

"Rad, seriously, you have got to be kidding. Why are you being intimidated by a young boy? I'll admit that Zach has a reason to be protective. You know for a long time it was just me and Zach. Same difference with India. Both of my children get and need a certain amount of attention from me. Zach, because he's my firstborn and only son, India because she's a girl, and as a mother, I want to be careful of who I allow around her—or them for that matter. Being a single mother, I was and still am very protective of both of them. After all, I'm all they have. I hope that's not a problem for you, honey," Bria replied.

"It's not a problem for me. I would never do anything to harm your children. I have kids of my own, so I understand. I'm just talking 'bout what I'm talkin' 'bout that's all. Zach seems to be the one with the problem. Just watch, you'll see."

Several days had gone by since Bria last talked to Lynette and had given her an update on how the relationship was going with Rad due to all the time she was spending with him. Bria had been thinking about the discussion she and Rad had regarding Zach and felt it was time to get Lynette's take on it. She made it a point and called her friend to meet her for breakfast for girl talk and to catch up.

They decided on the Denny's restaurant on Sandy Hollow Road so they would be near the bypass, which meant easy access to Cherryvale Mall just in case they wanted to do some shopping afterward. As Bria pulled into the parking lot, she noticed Lynette's black Monte Carlo parked near a front stall. Bria found a spot alongside Lynette's car, parked, got out the car and walked in the front entrance. There appeared to be a crowd waiting as Bria neared the doors, so she looked through to see if Lynette was already seated. As Bria poked her head through the crowd, she noticed Lynette at a booth near a window and proceeded to walk over to greet her.

"Hey, girlfriend. I didn't mean to keep you waiting long. What are you having?" Bria asked, scooting into the booth.

"I think I'll have my usual—pancakes, eggs, bacon and sausage," Lynette said, perusing the menu.

"*Hmmm,* that sounds good. I guess I'll go for the chicken fajita skillet with pancakes on the side," Bria said.

"You ladies need more time?" asked the approaching slender dark-skinned waitress.

"No. I'm ready if you are, Bri," Lynette said.

"So am I."

Bria and Lynette gave their orders.

"Girl, you know how we always said how we wished we had listened to our mothers when they told us to wait until marriage and the whole nine before having kids and yada?" Bria asked.

"*Umm-hmm.* You know I do. I say it myself all the time," Lynette said.

"Rad was saying a few nights ago that he thinks Zach is having a problem with our relationship. I can't see it. You know Rad and Zach always seem to have some sort of dissension going on. I hate to think Rad is jealous of my kids. I mean he just needs to realize my kids mean the world to me. I'll do anything for them," Bria said.

"Yeah, girl. I hear you. Your kids are a package deal, that's for sure. The men always seem to compete with the kids though. I don't know why that is. You want to be with them both—the kids and the men," Lynette said.

"Right, but I'll tell you what, my kids are my priority. If the man can't see that, then his ass better get to steppin'," Bria said.

The two ladies laughed and slapped each other a high five.

"But seriously, do you ever think what it would have been like to have just stayed with Leon or Stetson?" Lynette asked Bria.

"Let me say this: First of all, I have no regrets about having my children. Second of all, had I stayed with Leon, India wouldn't be here, so I say that...yeah, I think about it, then I quickly think about how Leon and I were too young. He didn't know how to be a daddy, let alone be a husband. Remember, my family tried to get me to marry him back when they found out I was pregnant? I, on the other hand, realized I was stupid, but I wasn't that damn stupid to marry his ass. Hell naw...

"As I see it, he wasn't really there for me or my son. I would have been miserable. As for Stetson, yeah he took care of us financially, but that man had started talking to me like my opinions didn't matter. I liked that he accepted Zach as his own, and even after India was born, Stetson never made any difference between the two kids, so yeah that was nice. Things were good for a while...we were like a normal family. The major issue was of course Stetson didn't want to work legitimately, let's not forget that. Even though he didn't sell out of our home, drug dealing wasn't exactly the occupation to be proud of or secure for that matter. I had to get out of that situation—should have never been in it. Especially not with kids involved," Bria said.

"I hear you. We can get passed those previous relationships, but our babies are here to stay. I asked you that question 'cause I think about it all the time. I guess what it amounts to is I feel I made some really bad choices in men, and now I am paying for it, and I don't want my girls to suffer because of my mistakes. Whoever I allow in my life or around my children has to be a positive. But getting back to Zach, do you think it's anything to be concerned with? Have you tried to talk to him about this? You know Zach has always been so laid back about things. Even as a little boy he was just content playing with his toy men and cars—always so happy-go-lucky," Lynette said.

"No. I haven't really talked to Zach about this yet because I haven't seen evidence of any real problem firsthand. I just think it's that Zach isn't ready for anyone to take Stetson's place yet. What he doesn't know is Stetson isn't making any effort to see him. It's been a while since we've had a man doing the things around the house that Rad does when he's there. I just think Zach feels like Rad is moving in on his territory. I'm hoping things will work out, and in time Zach sees there's room for both of them. I think he'll be alright," Bria said.

"So how does India seem to get along with Rad?" Lynette asked.

"Oh, now little miss thang can be a trip too. India has always demanded attention, and now that all eyes aren't on her, she does get passively aggressive. I know I have those kids slightly spoiled. That's the one regret I have as a single mom, but still as long as I don't see any abuse from the man to my kids, I don't believe there's an issue. I keep one eye open. I like Rad, but I'm not a fool, especially when it comes to my kids. I haven't seen any signs of perversion from Rad. I won't tolerate that type of B.S.

"What I do see is a battle for territory, like affection and time from me to the kids. Rad will come over and both of the kids and I are piled in my bed watching a movie, and the kids are laying on me. Sometimes you can feel the uneasiness in the room. Then, on the other hand, there are times when Rad is already present and both of us are watching a movie or whatever and snuggling close then Zach and India do all they can to literally bust us up. I mean they'll be in the other room tearing up shit or making all sorts of noise. It's crazy. When it's just me, Zach and India at home, you can hear a pin drop. They're both content hanging out in their room. You know you think you're doing the right thing by bringing someone into their lives who makes us all a normal family, then you just don't know what you should do at times. I just wish I had all the answers to being a good parent. Sometimes I just don't want to play anymore, but I know that isn't an option," Bria said.

"You're right, girl. It's not at this point. Yeah, I think the kids are a little jealous of Rad getting your attention. You just need to reassure them that you love them both and that no man can re-place the love you have for them," Lynette said.

"You're right. It's so funny how those kids do. I still make sure I have quality time with each of them. Not only that, but Rad and I include them in things as well. It's just so complicated sometimes."

"Hang in there, girl. Life itself is complicated at times, but you know we're survivors. We don't give up without a fight," Lynette said.

"I know, girl. I know. Sometimes I just get tired of the fight. We as African-American women have enough struggles—our homes, our jobs, our finances. I don't know if I could have made it had I been born during the Civil Rights era," Bria said.

"You and me either," Lynette agreed.

"Speaking of our jobs, did you put in for that position at work?" Bria asked.

"As a matter of fact, last week at the Eldorado Club for Dee Jenkins' relocating party, I met the manager of the call center, and as it turns out, Dee worked for him last year. Girl, it pays to network, so after we were introduced, I happened to mention I had applied for the position in his department. He promised he would personally pull my application and have his assistant give me a call sometime later this week," Lynette said.

"Girl, we've been sitting here, and I've been going on and on about my trivial drama. Why didn't you stop me and share your good news with me before I dumped all my stuff on you? That's good news. I'm so happy for you," Bria said.

"No problem. We're friends, that's what I'm here for—I listen to your stuff, you listen to mine. We're good. But yeah...I just don't want to get too excited about it. The position won't actually be ready until four months from now."

"Right, and we know how fast four months can go by. Well, hard work pays off, and good things come to those who believe and achieve, and I'm sure something good will come out of this. I mean really, what were the chances of you meeting the manager at Dee's party? I say that's divine intervention. Who knew the manager would be there, better yet who knew you put in for that position other than me 'cause I know how private you are about your career moves...so am I. That wasn't just some coincidence. You go, girl. That position is yours," Bria said.

"I hope you're right. There's just some details I left out though. During our introduction, he looked at me as if we had met before. Dee introduced us, and he took my hand. I, of course, expected a cordial handshake but no, the guy held my hand soooo long and said, 'So you're Lynette. So glad to meet you.' I was starting to feel somewhat awkward and the man was *still* holding my hand," Lynette said.

"*Hmmph*...Wonder what that was about," Bria said.

"I don't know, but I'll keep you posted."

By this time, the two ladies had finished their meals as the waitress slid the bill on their table.

"Shoot, look at the time. Girl, I've gotta get going. No shopping for me today. I forgot I told Dale I would have the car back by noon," Lynette said.

"Works for me, honey. I don't have any extra money for shopping, although that ain't never stopped us before. Anyhow, I need to spend some quality time with the kids, especially Zach so I can find out what's in his head."

Bria took her napkin, wiped her mouth, took a drink of water, then slid out the booth.

"Come on let's go. I've got the bill this time. Keep me posted about that job though. That's got me curious," Bria said.

Both ladies departed the restaurant and went their individual ways.

Bria was consumed with so much past baggage—the shame from her childhood, promiscuity, hurt, pain and insecurity. She hid her true feelings by jumping from relationship to relationship, yet she always thought she had the children's best interest at heart. In June 1987, despite all her doubts, Bria married Rad as soon as he breathed the proposal, which was six months after they met. The excuse she used was she would not waste six years with another man like she had done with Stetson.

Bria was pregnant when they got married, and by the end of the year, she gave birth to a third child, a daughter they named Shea. Feeling almost normal since this was the first time Bria birthed a child in wedlock with the father present, she thought her life was complete. Bria felt all she needed to break a family curse—or so she called it. Realizing she had seen too often single parenting in her own family, she was bound and determined to be married at least one time in life and raise her children in a two-parent home.

Because Bria didn't get the emotional attention and support needed during her childhood, she was fixated on what she believed was the normal family structure, which was why she settled for most of what she allowed in her marriage to Rad. Growing up and being preoccupied in her dysfunctional home with Bea made it hard for Bria to know how to get her needs met as an adult woman and not having her father around made it difficult to know how to establish healthy relationships with men.

There were some good times, but thinking back, she realized there were some things she had purposely overlooked when they were married. Even before they were married, she dismissed the fact that one of his aunts had said right in front of her to Rad, "Boy, I hope you don't mess over that girl 'cause you know you ain't no earthly good."

Bria heard the aunt but never once did she bother to ask why the woman had made the comment.

The second red flag was Rad was unemployed for most of the time he and Bria dated, claiming he had previously been laid off and was receiving unemployment benefits while diligently seeking future employment.

Red flag three: Bria learned the car he had been driving the night of their meeting didn't belong to him. The truth had been Rad didn't even own his own vehicle. He had claimed he had recently been in an accident that totaled his car and that he was awaiting an insurance settlement. She later learned he had been driving the automobile of one of his buddies who had allowed Rad to use the car as a favor. Bria overlooked many of Rad's indiscretions since the times they spent together seemed priceless. Rad had a way of doting over Bria that made her feel very special as a woman. He was very attentive to her in public and seemed to be her knight in shining armor, which she longed for—that is, if there was such a thing.

Bria never doubted that Rad loved his baby girl, despite the fact he had made it clear he didn't want any more children because he had two other children from two previous relationships. He contradicted himself by saying if he ever had any more kids he wanted it to be a boy. Bria thought, *Right. Like I really have control over that.* She sensed Rad did everything to convince himself his daughter wouldn't be a punk, which was what he had so often stated. Bria felt he had purposely set out to make Shea tough. Bria reminisced how Rad would dote over Shea and take Shea everywhere with him. If Bria had only known some of the environments Rad had taken their baby girl, she would have literally screamed.

Eventually, Bria noticed a change in dynamics between Rad, Zach and India. For one thing, Rad acted overly possessive of Shea at home when he shielded her from Bria's other two children and insisted on the kids wearing hospital masks whenever they were around the infant. Bria went along with it, not realizing the level of resentment this created with the kids. She was blinded by her fixation to create an illusionary family that she would go along with just about anything Rad said.

When Zach and India asked why Rad treated them differently Bria would dismiss it by saying he was looking out for the best interest of Shea because she had been a sickly baby who they hadn't wanted to risk becoming sicker. In her mind though, she knew that was a lie. She just didn't have any other reason for his behavior and hadn't wanted to admit that she might have made another poor choice.

But as time went on, Rad's negativity toward the kids got so obvious she could no longer ignore it. She figured one solution to the growing problems was for Zach and India to get to know their biological fathers. She tried to contact Leon and Stetson individually to no avail. Leon repeatedly broke promises to get Zach and always failed to follow through as it related to commitments with Zach. Stetson was good at bringing India material things but spent very little to no quality time with either child even though he considered Zach his own.

After several attempts to incorporate the fathers into their children's lives, Bria gave up, and by then, it was too late. Zach wasn't at all interested in forming any relationship with Leon, and Bria realized she would be forcing her child to forge a relationship with someone he simply did not know. Instead, she started filling Zach's fatherless void with material things and outings, such as skating, boys club activities, sleepovers with his friends, and just about anything to consume his time to make him happy.

India was now six and seemed to care less either way so long as her mother was giving her attention by buying her pretty clothes, Barbie dolls, Cabbage Patch dolls, or stuffed Care Bears. Each time Bria was pregnant after Zach she struggled with feelings of not having enough love to provide for yet another child.

In fact, it had amazed her how much she loved each one of her children who meant the world to her. It hurt her that Rad was trying to destroy what she had longed for—a healthy, loving environment for her children.

The pain became too much to bear, and she could no longer ignore the constant dissension in her home. It had gotten to a point where Zach and India started acting out, which resulted in her yelling and cursing at the kids similar to what Bea did with her. The more she tried to talk to Rad about it, the worse it got as he continued to say she was putting the kids before their marriage, and he accused the kids of being spoiled.

Bria felt so helpless and didn't know what to do next, but she knew she had to do something as Zach had started taking his frustrations out on her, and so was India. Bria had started reading self-help books to get herself through the rough periods in her life, and she got involved in church, even though Rad refused to attend. Even though her faith in God grew stronger, she wondered if the kids, especially Zach, could benefit from some type of counseling because he seemed so withdrawn and angry toward her. One day when they were alone, she asked Zach if he would like to talk to someone.

His response was, "You need counseling, I don't. I'm normal. Ain't nothing wrong with me. I don't want to talk to nobody. Y'all go ahead, just leave me alone. I'm okay."

Startled by the maturity of her young son's response, she thought it was just better to leave it alone and never brought it up again.

Chapter Six

BRIA HAD BEEN THE TYPE of friend who was good at listening and giving advice, but as it related to her own circumstances, she had a difficult time making the right choice. She was a kind caring person who became engulfed in her close friends issues at times while ignoring her own needs.

Over and over in her mind she replayed the last conversation she'd had with Lynette about Rad's actions toward Zach

I don't know why I didn't see the signs. I should have listened to Zach more closely. I'm sure he was telling me something about Rad. I just didn't want to face it—couldn't see it at the time, Bria thought. *Nine years later, and now I have not two but three children.*

Bria and Rad had many ups and downs during their marriage. Bria had realized sooner than she cared to admit she shouldn't have married Rad, but she had allowed things to move so quickly between them that she didn't want to back out due to embarrassment.

In retrospect, she believed had she had the courage, she should have cut her losses and ran from the relationship.

His debonair, cunning nature had wooed her. Bria had ignored all the obvious signs all the way from the beginning of the relationship. Rad told her he was in between jobs when they met, and even though she had her own suspicions about it, she had accepted his lie—he wasn't working nor had he been laid off, and as she thought about it, to make matters even worse, he did not have a Computer Numerical Control operator certification as he had claimed. CNC operators generally earned decent wages, so she was impressed. All she thought at the time was he was appealing and very well versed, so why not give the brother a chance.

During their early courtship, Rad too was open, kind and seemed sincere, he had shared some things about his past that preyed on her emotional sensitivity because she was vulnerable coming out of the relationship with Stetson. Bria felt safe with him because when they were together in public, he always grabbed her hand and guided her through the crowd, unlike some of her friends and their men, who when they were out, the guy just walked separately from his lady. Bria thought that Rad was a protector who was attentive, so she believed that sealed the deal—or as Bea would say, it was the icing on the cake. She did not want to have yet another child out of wedlock, so against her better judgment—or better yet stupidity—Bria agreed to marry Rad.

In the beginning, things seemed tolerable. Rad was receiving unemployment benefits. He lied and told Bria he gave up his Cadillac so he could provide for her and help out with the family expenses, so they shared her car. No problem. It all seemed to make sense—at first until the lies began to unravel.

Rad was his own version of a stay-at-home dad. He would on occasion prepare a meal and babysit Shea while Bria worked. Two years into the marriage, sporadically when Rad decided to work, things would change temporarily. Rad seemed to keep a job long enough to appease Bria, just to get her off his back, to alleviate the nagging and so on, then he'd find some reason why he got let go.

This pattern repeated itself randomly throughout the marriage. Just when Bria let her guard down and trusted him, he let her down. She lost count of the times she and the kids waited on him to show up from work some evenings and later into the early hours of the following morning. Eventually, Rad would show up giving various excuses for emergencies that supposedly caused his delay in coming home. These scenarios lasted off and on for approximately seven years. By then, Bria had grown weary and tired of trying to save their marriage, and that was about the time she got evidence Rad was using drugs. Bria also discovered financial discrepancies and signs of other women Rad had been with—pictures and phone numbers. But she finally lost her patience in 1996 when nine-year-old Shea asked Bria one day why her little brother couldn't visit their home.

"What little brother, Shea?" Bria asked.

"Me and my daddy always have to go over to his house," Shea complained.

"Over to his house? Whose house? What the hell are you talking about, Shea?"

Bria was barely able to comprehend what she had just heard from her young daughter.

"My brother, Justin. I'm tired of going over there all the time," Shea went on.

"Who is your little brother, Shea, and where does he live? Who is his mother, and who told you have a little brother?" Bria could sense a headache coming on as she quizzed her child.

"My daddy told me not to tell you. I have a picture of him too. I can show you the house where he lives if you drive there 'cause me and my daddy go over there all the time. Do you want to see it? He doesn't live that far from here," Shea said.

"What the...? Yeah, show me the picture first then show me the house. Okay, let me calm down. This is too damn much right now. How about we go for a ride? Do you think you could show me where your little brother lives?"

"Okay, Mommy, but you have to promise you won't tell my daddy I told you. He'll be mad at me if I tell 'cause he said this was our secret. So, you have to promise me you won't tell him. You promise?" Shea pleaded.

"Girl, you can tell your momma anything, and I won't say a word, okay?"

Bria hated to have to lie to Shea, but she knew that would be the only way to obtain the information. Bria got nauseous after she looked at the picture of the little boy. His skin tone, nose, cheekbones and lips all resembled Rad.

Bria and Shea rode north of their brick bungalow two blocks away. Bria never imagined she would be playing detective with her baby girl Shea leading her to the location of her husband's mistress and their illegitimate child. Bria's heart was racing. She could feel herself breathing faster, and the headache was more intense as she outwardly tried to remain unnerved by her inward emotions. Not knowing what to expect, Bria envisioned seeing Rad's black Chrysler Fifth Avenue parked along the street or in the driveway of one of the houses lining the street. Bria reduced the speed of the vehicle, driving very slowly so Shea could identify the inconspicuous location.

"Are you sure this is the street, Shea?" Bria asked.

"I'm pretty sure 'cause of that thing in that yard over there," Shea answered, referring to near life-size replica of Michelangelo's David in the front yard of one of the homes.

"Why in the hell would someone want that gaudy thing in their yard?" Bria whispered, not really expecting an answer.

"*Hmmm.* It's kind of hard to see since it's so dark out here," Shea said.

"Don't you and your dad usually come here during the nighttime?" Bria asked.

"Naw. It's mostly in the daytime when you're at work and after he gets me from school," Shea innocently replied.

"I see, so it's too dark for you to tell which house you visit. Well, I'll go real slow to give you time to figure it out, but you are sure this is the correct street?"

"Yeah, 'cause of that thing," Shea answered, pointing to the statue.

Bria and Shea rode up and down the street at least three

more times. Shea acted as if she couldn't remember the exact home, pointing out two to three different possibilities but not being certain. Bria decided it was best to surrender the cause and head back home. Besides, her headache had worsened, and there was no telling what the outcome would be in the revelation.

Days passed after she and Shea ventured out to find the little brother's home. Bria had not said anything to Rad about what Shea had told her. Instead, she recounted the opportunities Rad had to get away with his infidelities—the betrayal, signs that were there but through denial she dismissed or simply ignored. Bria had so many questions going through her mind. For starters, she began to wonder why she had been so gullible and allowed herself to be betrayed. She saw the signs almost from the beginning. Nearly ten years was way too long to be subjected to such a relationship. She felt it was because of her own insecurities and low self-esteem.

She recalled something she had learned in one of the many self-help books she began reading while going through the co-dependency classes she attended while Rad was in rehab once. Paraphrased, it had to do with individuals losing self-identity when so much focus was placed on pleasing other people. Bria knew she had been guilty of being a people pleaser and an enabler. As a child Bria had learned to take on the negative consequences of Bea's behavior and cover it up or make excuses for it to family, friends or anyone on the outside to prevent public shame. In some passive controlling sort of way, she believed she could change how people acted toward her if she showed them enough love. But Bria ended up feeling sad and neglected due to wasted time and energy spent on these individuals.

She met Rad and found out through their getting-to-know-you conversations that he had a similar background. Wanting to be safe and remain in her social class, she thought Rad was the man for her. She didn't realize that one doesn't have to remain in one's past. Just because one was raised a certain way or from a certain background doesn't mean one has to remain that way. Society has people believing they are nothing if they weren't raised with a silver spoon in their mouths. It took her a long time to realize this for herself. She had always been a hard worker. The one thing she decided to do was to be better than the situation she was in. One step at a time, she began her plan. First things first, Rad had to go and would no longer be a part of her future as it related to having a man in her life

Bria was still confidentially keeping the information Shea had confided in her. Days had passed. She was careful not to bring up the subject in front of the child. She was trying to weigh out the worst-case scenario. She didn't want to jeopard-ize the trust her daughter had placed in her, yet she grew angry and resentful as she began to think about Rad using their child in such a precarious situation. What he actually had done was taught their child to lie at a young age by keeping such a secret from her mother.

Going through the motions of their daily rituals, she finally got the courage to confront Rad about what Shea had told her. Naturally, Rad denied everything, saying Shea had made the story up. She informed him that Shea had given her a picture of her so-called brother. When confronted with the picture, Rad insisted the little boy belonged to his brother Jock and became adamant he had the picture because it was his nephew. That was the story he stuck to. Rad even went as far as calling Jock on the phone to confirm his side of the story. Confused and conned again, she believed him. Then one day, their home phone rang, and not realizing she had picked up, Rad answered. She heard another woman whisper, "You miss me, baby?"

The caller must have thought Rad didn't hear her the first time, so she repeated the question: "You miss me, baby?"

Still silence. He must have been trying to determine whether Bria was nearby.

"We miss you. Are we going to see you today?" the caller asked.

Bria froze in place. She felt her blood pressure rise immediately upon hearing another woman's voice on the other end of the phone questioning her own husband. Bria wondered if what she was hearing was real or if she misheard something, then she heard Rad say in a low voice, "What are doing calling me here? She's home."

By that time, she had already started tiptoeing from the kitchen to the bedroom, phone receiver in tow, to ease upon Rad from behind as he unknowingly continued speaking lower hovering over the phone. She had muted the background noises and held the phone she was carrying to her own ear, first grabbing a plastic serving spoon from the kitchen counter. Without further hesitation, she hit him on the top of his bald head using the plastic base of the serving spoon, not once, not twice, but in a rage, not thinking of any repercussions. By this time, Rad hung up the phone with the other woman as soon as he realized Bria was in the room.

"You bastard. Get out, you lying bastard. Who was that bitch calling my house? Was that your son's mother? Don't bother answering, Rad. I know more than I need to know. Enough is enough. It's not enough that I've put up with your drug usage and going back and forth with different jobs. Now this. Aren't I worth more than this? I'm not putting up with your shit. Get the hell out. There's nothing you can say to me. Get the hell out."

Rad grabbed at his head and the spoon as he tried to dodge any more hits yelling, "Girl, you're crazy. That's somebody with a wrong number. Stop hitting me like you done lost your mind. What are you doing?"

"I'm doing what I should have done a long time ago. I'm getting all of your shit and you out of here," Bria said.

He grabbed her wrist and twisted the spoon from her hand, then he bear hugged her from behind and tossed her onto the bed.

"Girl, you'd better quit hitting me like you're crazy. I told you that was a wrong number."

"Wrong number? Wrong number, Rad? Who do you think I am, Booboo the Fool?"

"Girl, I can't control who calls this house. Why you don't believe me? Who was it then?"

"Rad, I don't know the bitch's name, but it was no wrong number. I know that for damn sure. I'll tell you the wrong number. The wrong number was when I let you woo my ass in the first place. That was the wrong number. You would be better off saying you got caught up when you were off on one of your highs. That would be better than you trying to insult my intelligence by telling me that was a wrong number. Why should I believe you? I heard you say 'why are you calling me here. She's home.' Why would you say that to a wrong number? I guess your stupid ass didn't know what all I heard. You know what? I guess you hung up on her when you heard me, huh? Well, call the bitch back and tell her she don't have to miss you no more 'cause you're on your way. I'll help you get your shit and get the hell out of here. I should have been through with your ass when I found your damn work shoes on the top of my refrigerator. Who does that? You had to be high that night...but nooo, I believed that story about you being so tired from work that you didn't realize where you put your shit."

"Girl, you're crazy. I'm going out before you make me hurt you."

"Yeah, the day you put your hands on me will be the day you never forget. I know you better get out of my face now or you won't be able to sleep at night."

Rad left the house that night, but he came back as he normally would, thinking Bria was asleep. Rad was an addict, so when Bria said leave, that gave him the reason he needed to go get high without her knowing. Bria was so used to being co-dependent that she allowed him to go and come. Even when she said leave, most times she let him come back. This time Rad entered the rear door into the kitchen. Bria was sitting and waiting for him at the table. She had had enough and calmly convinced Rad to leave for good and to take some of his things.

That next day, she went to Ace hardware store and bought new locks for all the outside doors. On the way home, she stopped at IGA grocery store and asked the store manager for cardboard boxes so she could pack the remainder of Rad's things. She knew he had to go. She arrived home where she met Jim her handyman whom she'd called. Jim changed all the locks and didn't ask any questions. Friday, she saw an attorney with whom she consulted to begin her divorce proceedings. Before the divorce was final, she had heard through the grapevine that Rad had moved in with the mother of his child.

When things with him were finally over, she presumed he did what he thought he had to do in order to get back at her and to show her what a man he was. He was seen more out in public with his other woman and son.

She thought, *Guess he got his son after all.*

By May 1997, the divorce from Rad was final. Bria learned the hard way that she had no control over other people. She took time to reevaluate her life and all she had gone through. Bria could not undo the past or any previous mistakes. She was reflecting on how to move on. In her mind, she began to change how she saw her life. Everyone had choices. She started a mental process of formulating the necessary steps to refocus, reshape, and recharge her life.

For so long, something had been missing, and she asked herself why had she allowed herself to be neglected, mistreated, and disrespected. She once had dreams, but now she was faced with what they were, what was her purpose, and what should she do now. Bria was tired and weary but at the same time was a fighter who did not believe in giving up. Knowing she had the children and wanting to be a good example for them, Bria pulled herself together. She had decided her life was more valuable and she would take responsibility for her choices, learn from the past, and be empowered to move forward. She was tired of trying to live up to the expectations of others, particularly the men in her life. Time had shown most of the men in her life, including the one man she sought so long to please—her own father—had let her down.

Finally, after the heartbreak, the letdown, she still found herself unfulfilled because not yet had she begun to seek anything that really contributed to her individual personal growth. After years of much contemplation, she conscientiously decided something in her life must change. She had given Rad nine years of her life. She had always been committed in one way or another to another human being since the age of sixteen. Figuring she had come from a single-parent home with an alcoholic mother, father married to another woman, and born out of wedlock, she had always thought she was unworthy of anything or anyone of a certain caliber.

Bria was totally devastated after the breakup with Rad and struggled for a while to pick up the pieces to her life. She didn't know where to start, but she knew she had to start somewhere. She withdrew into her children, her job, and church. It took some time, but she grew stronger and realized she was better off without Rad and relationships period for a while, and she wondered why it had taken her so long to make the change.

Bria thought back over the years of her life up to present in a matter of moments. Thinking aloud, she said, "There are so many things I could have done differently."

Trying to pick up the pieces of her life, Bria re-enrolled in community college to once again to try to finish her associate's degree in business. She had made several attempts—one when she initially graduated high school back in 1978, then again at least on three other occasions. Among the excuses were needing more income to care for Zach, not enough time, a new position at work, and school being too overwhelming. It was 1997, nineteen years had passed. Bria had procrastinated. She was now thirty-five, but no matter how long it took, it was a major accomplishment for her to complete school. There had always been something inside her that nagged at her spirit to finish what she had started so many years ago. She vowed to complete school even if it meant being a forty-five-year-old graduate. She had finally resolved to do something meaningful for her life. Her goal was to get an associate's degree then transfer to a university for a bachelor's degree, then ultimately get a master's degree.

Having a degree had always been her desire. Bria felt so confident when she was in school. She just didn't know why it took her so long to attain her goal. What was it that left her unmotivated when she wanted so much and needed to complete her lifelong goal? One thing was certain: It was imperative to be a role model for her children, so if for no other reason, the insecurities or whatever, she was determined to complete her education. She thought more about Zach while shutting off the computer and closing the *Principles of Micro Economics* textbook.

Bria had grown stronger in her faith and confidence, and she believed she was in a good place in her life. She and the children joined a new church and became active in activities, like choir, youth of today auxiliaries and other social functions to maintain a healthy and active life. Since the divorce from Rad, she had decided to take baby steps to repair her life. She was on journey to become a better role model for her children and to focus on bettering her life. Just when she thought things had been running along fairly well and she was finally getting her and the children's lives back on track, out of nowhere came another blow. For a while, there had been no serious family drama, so she thought, *Thank God. Lord knows, I have been through enough.*

Chapter Seven

WITH ALL THAT HAD BEEN going on, life didn't stop and the children were getting older. Zach was now twenty-one, India was sixteen, and Shea was nine. Bria thought she had let Zach down in some ways because there had not been a positive male figure in Zach's life. As she reflected on the past, it all seemed a blur because she couldn't pinpoint where the time had gone. She and the children existed in a home for years with a man who was always vying for Bria's time and causing a wedge between her relationship with Zach and India.

Bria knew that was time she couldn't get back but realized she needed to zoom in on what Zach needed to be a sustainable adult in life. She couldn't help but think of what she felt was one of the biggest pitfalls for Zach. Bria used to always jokingly say she could have had ten sons like Zach because coming up he was always so laid back, kind, and respectful, and he never fell prey to peer pressure like some of the other young boys his age who were sometimes in and out of trouble. Zach was content with playing sports, going to the boys clubs, hanging out with friends, skating, and other social activities. The biggest concern Bria had for Zach was he lacked the drive needed to set and reach his goals.

It had been touch and go getting him done with high school because of some of his grades, but with the help of some teachers and Bria's intervention, Zach managed to complete school on time, graduating with his class. But he didn't have a plan for what to do next. Bria had tried to get him enrolled in one of the technical IT schools. He didn't want to do that, so she took him to all of the Army, Navy, and Marine military recruiters office. He refused that, so she and Zach settled on him working for a while until he figured out what it was he would do with his life. In Bria's opinion, she really wanted him to go into the military believing that would give him the life skills to be a man he didn't get coming up. She knew it had to be Zach's decision so she left it alone. Zach got a full-time job and moved out.

Bria also thought a lot of what Zach was dealing with had to do with the lack of involvement from his father, but Zach would never admit that and would not want to discuss it when she brought it up. Bria tried to reach Zach, but he would shut her down. She knew he was struggling with issues but couldn't seem to reach him. This was one of the major pitfalls Bria observed with her son, but he was twenty-one now, so he decided he would have to figure it out.

"That girl done been here before" was what Bria's mother, Bea, would always say about any child who to Bea acted too grown up for their age. Bea made that comment about India frequently.

Bria didn't see India as a precocious child but described her as one who was outspoken and somewhat too mature for her age. By the same token, out of all the kids, Bria and India were a lot alike, which was one reason she believed they clashed so much. Bria had watched India grow up, and most of what India had gone through had been very similar to her own life experiences. She could read India like a book.

In India's pre-teen years, she would plot and scheme just to hang out without permission with her girlfriends. India and her young girlfriends used any reason conceivable to get out the house. For all Bria knew, they were enjoying skating outings, slumber parties, and movies, but that wasn't the case. India wanted to be where the boys were. She wanted to be where the action was is what India had said to her mother in later years. Many times, India's behavior caused a push-and-pull relationship between Bria and India because Bria thought India should be using her time more wisely. The more she encouraged India to do things like studying, reading, or cheerleading—things that would shape her character into a responsible adult—the more India rebelled. Bria had a bad feeling of what India was doing and what it could lead to and tried to convince her there would be plenty of time for boys, but India didn't want to hear that.

It wasn't that Bria was unrealistic. She understood India's attraction to the opposite sex. She just thought it was a bit too soon because India was too young. It appeared India was overly obsessed by the attention from the boys. The reality was as a toddler, India seemed to require specialized individual attention period, but this was something Bria had not stopped to think about until much later. Looking back, Bria regretted she had spent so much time trying to have a regular family by thinking they needed a man to complete them. As hard as she worked to provide for her family, Bria blamed herself for the hours she spent commuting to a job feeling unappreciated when she could have spent quality time with her children. She thought she was doing the right thing then, but she never took the time to ask the children how they felt.

As Bria watched her children grow up, she reminisced about the past and constantly blamed herself for the children's life-styles and for the choices they made. Maybe India did suffer from lack of attention. That could be why India at age sixteen, like Bria, ended up being a teenaged mother, giving birth to Bria's first grandchild. Bria managed to get through the obstacle of teenage motherhood with India by guiding her through school and ensuring she did not quit school. India became very studious and graduated at the top of her class. After graduating, India got a full-time job and enrolled in the community college. But like Bria, India did not sacrifice going to school over working to provide a decent living for her child. India was very driven and always excelled in working her way up to some sort of management position at whatever company she worked for.

Six years later, it was Bria, India, Shea and India's baby trying to make it. Life had been no bed of roses for Bria, but they made the best of what life had to offer. It was 2003. Time didn't wait on anyone, and Bria would always say, "If you're doing nothing, time will always pass, so you might as well be found doing something productive."

No one could have ever told Bria what life's experiences had in store for her next. Bria felt like she had been sucker punched in her gut for the first time in her forty-three years. She was totally caught off guard by bits and pieces of a conversation she overheard while eavesdropping like a thief in the night on the stairwell of her own home. She was still trying desperately to process what she'd heard and at the same time dismiss it.

Bria was having a hard time understanding why her younger daughter was making references to the person on the other end of her phone of not being scared to be seen with her. Bria wondered who *her* was and to what Shea was referring. Bria thought she heard Shea say something about a kiss—"I did it 'cause I wanted to" and "yeah, I did like it," "I will do you next time," "I promise. Yes, I will."

What was she talking about and to whom was she talking? It sounded like a girl, because Bria heard her say "girl, you crazy," but at the same time, it sounded like a relationship or courtship conversation. Bria knew she should have burst into the room and demanded an explanation, but she was frozen in place, not wanting to have to address what she was hearing. Bria didn't know what to do.

Bria had almost lost her composure. She had to reach deep within herself to pull it together. Bria pulled it together when she heard her daughter make a reference that she heard a noise because Shea said something like, "Girl, let me get off this phone to see where my mom is." That's when Bria quietly crept down the stairs to her own room.

For weeks, she had shared her suspicions about her daughter's behavior to her best friend, Harmony Starr, but never did she imagine it would be something as unbearable as what she heard. She wondered how she would muster up the strength to pull herself together before she confirmed her painful revelation with Harmony. But she could not shake the nagging thoughts that repeatedly invaded her mind like gnats over a bowl of fruit. As hard as she tried to shake the memory of the overheard conversation of her sixteen year-old daughter, she couldn't.

Bria had been up long past her regular bedtime. She knew her mind was consumed with thoughts of her personal life. As she continued to stare at the laptop, she realized she was particularly thinking about her youngest daughter instead of completing an assignment for her online college course. Tears began to well in her eyes, and she felt defeated. She knew she had to go to bed and get rested for work the next day.

As she closed the laptop and prepared for bed, one thought after the other flooded her mind. *It seems like it was just yesterday my baby was born. Where did I go wrong? I shouldn't have been so strict with her.*

Bria had always prided herself on being a good mother to her three children—Zachary, India, and Shea. She had Zach at age sixteen, India at twenty-one, and Shea at twenty-seven. All the children had different fathers. She tried to prevent her girls from making some of the mistakes she had made along the way. She felt she might have come across as being a bit too hard sometimes because of how she was raised. She could not remember a time in her own childhood when she had choice of whether or not she followed her mother's rules, so Bria, being a young mother, had to learn most of what she knew about parenting the hard way.

All she knew for sure was that she did not want her kids to grow up like she had or in the type of environment she had been exposed to as a child. She thought she had considered her kids' feelings by allowing them a say-so when they disagreed on some of her home rules, and she eased up some. For one thing, she never disagreed with Bea when she was coming up or she would have been slapped in the mouth. Back in those days, what Bea said was gospel, and that was it. For that matter, no adult ever asked her how she felt about anything, so she tried to bring her children up differently—or so she thought.

It took a long time for her to get to that point. For so many years, she had not taken the time or effort to talk to the kids about how they felt, so she didn't know or understand their motives when they acted out. In her mind, it wasn't that she didn't love and care. She just hadn't been taught good mothering skills, and the example she had wasn't the best role model. What she knew she had to learn by trial and error.

Over the years, Bria had suffered painstaking guilt from her own experiences with promiscuity at a young age, so she was relentless when it came to protecting her girls. She thought being a good mother meant providing material things like clothes and shoes. She also provided money to the kids for privileges and liberties with their friends, such as going to the movies, having a teen phone line, which was long before cell phones in the days when the household had a land line and a secondary line called a teen phone. Bria always provided such, and a car, which were all things she had made sure she provided for them along the way.

In spite of her past bad relationships, she prided herself on raising her children in church, thinking that would be all they needed to keep them from bad influences and failures. Bria thought she was guarding them from the wrong people, places, and things when in fact she had sheltered them, which in some cases was a bigger disservice to the children since they had not been held accountable for anything. She did most everything for them—a lesson she had to learn the hard way.

She knew in her heart she was being overprotective at times, but that didn't matter to her, and the more she tried not to, the harm had already been done. After many years, she drew the conclusion that if she had been taught better, she would have done things differently.

All of what she knew from her past was why it was so difficult now, and over and over she couldn't get Shea's phone discussion out of her head. Her mental recorder vividly ran visuals of Shea playing outdoors along with the neighborhood kids as plain as day. By age nine, Shea had already taken an interest in basketball. She would ask to play the game until the streetlights came on. The temperature during the summer days in Rockford, Illinois, could be anywhere from the eighties and above and very humid. The kids were like nocturnal deer. They literally preferred to play outdoors under the illuminated streetlights of the city. It was during the dusk hours when the climate was cooler in the summer night. Typically, there was not much traffic up and down their narrow neighborhood street, and most of the parents on the block did not make a fuss about their kids being out at dusk. During that time, it was common for one of the neighborhood children to put a mobile basketball hoop and rim in the middle of the secluded street. To most parents on the block, it was an innocent and normal pastime for the youth, so they didn't mind them playing there. It never crossed Bria's mind that Shea was the only female in the group of boys shooting hoops. Instead, she thought it was safer than Shea running around with a bunch of fast girls doing who knows what.

On the flipside, Bria's older daughter, India, who was now twenty-two, had a different personality. At sixteen, Shea was very interested in school and the extracurricular activities of the time. India at sixteen wasn't interested at all in playing basketball like that. Bria thought it was interesting that each one of her children's personality differed from the other, and as their mother, it had made no difference to her one way or another. She loved them all unconditionally for who they were and had encouraged them to be their best selves and to excel at whatever they did. She hadn't realized that her two daughters would have such different personalities though they were both girls. Bria thought she knew all there was to know about young girls after raising India who had been full of surprises, but she soon learned there was still so much more to discover about raising girls and children.

Refocusing on the present, Bria was struggling to complete her homework at the computer. Her mind kept drifting with each stroke of the keyboard. Ten questions should not take three or four hours to complete, but tonight the review questions from her microeconomics class were taking her longer and longer to finish. She was startled by the phone ringing, abruptly awakening her to reality.

"Hello," Bria answered.

"Hey, girl. I was just calling to see if you were all right," Harmony Starr, Bria's best friend, replied.

"Hey, Harm. Yeah, girl. I'm hanging. I'm just trying to get my homework done so I can get my things ready for work tomorrow. I don't know what I was thinking when I decided to go back to school. It's been so long, and with this latest stuff happening in my life, I can barely concentrate, but I'm trying, I'm really trying."

"Well, keep at it, Bri. You know this is something you've been wanting for quite some time. Just because something happens in your life doesn't mean you're supposed to give up on everything and wallow through life with no purpose. I'm not trying to downplay what you're going through, but you know some things happen to make us stronger. This is just a test. You must ask yourself, will you do what it takes to pass. Girl, if I know you—and I do—you are strong enough, and I know you can make it through," Harmony said.

"Thanks, Harm. You know you've been there for me. But… girl, I didn't know you could preach too," Bria joked.

"I got it from you, girl. Don't start no mess now. I just need my friend to be alright. Well, I'm not going to keep you from your studies. Just wanted to call and check on you."

"Thanks, and yeah, I'm good. How are you doing? Where are the girls?" Bria asked.

"They're both in their rooms. Justice had to work, so she came in, took a shower and headed straight to bed. I told Tia to get away from me before I did something to her I would regret. That girl is always trying my patience," Harmony said.

"Yeah, they always do, don't they?" Bria commented.

"But other than that, we're just fine, nothing new—different day, same old, same old. Okay, so that's enough about my night...don't let me get into the humdrum of discussing my girls and our drama. I was just checking on you. I'm going to run now, so you go on and get back to your studies. We can talk to-morrow. Have a good night."

"You too, Harm. Talk to you later," Bria said.

Harmony and Bria had been friends for more than thirty years. The two ladies had met at the only factory job Bria had ever been employed and had been friends ever since.

When they met, Bria had Zach and India. Harmony only had Justice. The friends had been through first marriages and divorces. It was later in their friendship and other relationships that Shea was born to Bria, and Harmony had Tia. Bria had Shea from her first marriage. Harmony had Tia from a previous rela-tionship that failed. The friends had gone through so much to-gether—joy and pain, gas and light disconnections, bad credit, clunker cars, sparse kitchen cabinets to cooking together to make one meal and growing into womanhood together.

After Bria got off the phone with Harmony, she found herself thinking about the past as she would often do. She always won-dered had her upbringing been different would life have been better for her and the children.

"Whew, girl. Now I see why our mothers kept telling us not to be in a rush getting with boys and to wait until you get mar-ried to have kids," Bria said while visiting Harmony one day.

"Right. I know fo' damn well I wish I had listened," Harmony joked.

"These damn kids are so hard headed and just know everything already," Bria said.

"I sure don't feel like going through all this shit with Tia, sneaking out the damn house. Hell, I don't know where she got that shit from. I tried to break her damn neck when she walked through the door," Harmony said.

"I hear you, girl. I've taken all I could take from Shea. The last time I caught her coming in, I must have lost it. That girl walked in the door and right into my damn hand," Bria said.

"I know this: I'm not hiding anything around my house, and I'll dare Tia to try that shit again, sneaking out the house like she grown," Harmony said.

"Girl, makes you wonder why the Lord gives us this hard shit to deal with. I guess to make us stronger. What do you think?" Bria asked.

"I suppose but look like He should know we're pretty strong. Look at the stuff we've been through as single parents. Wasn't that enough?" Harmony reasoned.

"Yeah. Lord knows I've been through enough men and things in my life to know something. I can say this: We tried the best we could. All I wanted was what was best for my children. Sure, I made a few mistakes, but what parent doesn't? I didn't have a blueprint for parenting, especially not at my age. Sixteen was pretty young to have a child. Hell, I was still a child myself. But you know, Harm, the one thing I do try to instill in these kids is to at least grow up, and what I mean by that is for them to grow into their own person. Don't be one of these gullible-minded folks that don't think for yourself. Whatever or whoever you choose to be or do in life, hopefully positive, let it be your decision and not someone else's. That way if you falter, at least you're rooted and grounded in what you believe and have something to stand on."

"Bria, you know your ass is deep, girl, but you just said something very profound."

"Well, I don't know how profound it is, but it's what I firmly believe. One thing I can say about Bea is that she allowed me to experience life, and she wasn't afraid to let me make mistakes. When I made mistakes, she didn't beat me over the head with them. In her own way, she was right there for me when the shit didn't work out the way I thought it would. I appreciate her for that."

"I hear you, girlfriend."

"Sometimes I think about how Rad said he wanted a son. From the moment Shea was born, Rad didn't seem to embrace her feminine side. Hell, I remember one of her birthdays he bought her a boyish looking outfit. Sometimes I blame him for Shea being tomboyish."

"Look, Bria, I know you don't like what you heard about Shea's sexual preference and how the situation is being revealed right now, but she is still your baby girl. She has so much personality and character. You still must love your child, and honestly, I don't know that anyone is to blame. I personally believe Shea is too young to even understand who she is. It could be a fad—you know like peer pressure," Harmony said.

"Friend, I do love her, and I'm here for her, but I sure as hell don't understand her right now. I'm just being honest. I don't.

I'm trying not to let this weigh me down. It's like the less I know about it, the better for me right now. I need time to process it all, and as far as it being just a fad...well hell...I would rather she came in here with blue and pink hair than to start liking people of the same sex. Do you know how hard her life will be? It's my job to protect my babies from the cruelty of the world. What do you think people will say about her or even do to her? Let's change the subject. I want to hear about you. So have you decided whether or not to contact the Department of Vital Statistics?" Bria asked.

"Girl, yeah, I have. The girls keep asking me whether I want to know who my real mother and father are or were. I do. I'm especially curious every time we visit the doctor and have to complete the family medical history forms. Shit, I don't know what diseases or such medically is actually hereditary or what's not. Not only that, at the rate Tia is going, she might get with a relative and she not even know it. Hell, for that matter, maybe I have. It's something not knowing who your natural parents are," Harmony said.

"Girlfriend, you know I was just talking. I do understand the need to find your real people. You know how I feel about finding my real father. My only concern I have for you and me is that we find these people and they hurt us. Really, I'm not worried about me, but I don't want anyone to hurt you and Justice. I've been through much already, and I think I have pretty thick skin, but you and Justice, that's a whole different thing. You know I don't play when it comes to my friend. I'm very protective of you both," Bria said.

"I know it, and I love you like a sister, but I'm determined to find out. Believe me, I've thought about that too—all the what-ifs and the possibility of rejection—but like I said, I just want to know. It's not like I want anything from them. I just want some closure to this part of my life. You're right. I had two wonderful parents, so it has nothing to do with that. I just need to know," Harmony said.

"Remember how you told me about how your mother would say little things to you before she died? Seems like she was giving you clues in some ways to what you needed to know about your biological parents," Bria said.

"Oh yeah, thinking back, when I was real young, my mom did make minor references to my biological parents, but it made no difference to me then. I guess I wasn't ready to hear the details, so I would always brush it off and change the subject, it was like we went on to discuss something else. I guess it really didn't matter to me since I wasn't missing any nurturing or care. As far as I knew, she and my dad were my parents, so oh well. I might have asked her who my real momma and daddy were, but I can't even remember for sure if I asked. I guess I must have 'cause she did tell me she really didn't know for sure who my real parents were. She said she and my father got me from the Rockford Children's Home, and I was only a few months old at the time," Harmony said.

"So you were born in Rockford?" Bria asked.

"I guess so. All I know is that she said she worked for or with a lady who knew she and my dad weren't able to have children of their own, so this lady referred them to the Rockford Children's Home," Harmony said.

"The Rockford Children's Home. I haven't ever heard of it,"

Bria said.

"It's closed up now. Since Mama died, I tried contacting them and hit a dead end. I wanted to see if I could find out any information from their old records but wasn't able to. Then I was actually watching *Oprah* one day. Ironically, the topic was about people finding their adoptive parents. Actually, I hadn't even been paying attention to the show but caught the tail end as they were running the 800-number for finding adoptive parents. I jotted the number down, but like anything else, I put it off and didn't ever call," Harmony said.

One thing Bria knew about her friend was that when she set her mind to doing something, there was usually no stopping her. She knew when Harmony was ready, she would pursue finding her biological parents. Besides, she had enough on her hands with the burden of finding her own natural birth father.

"Yeah, girlfriend, when you put it in that perspective, I see what you mean. Certainly you had a good childhood, but I can see why you would want to know who your biological parents are," Bria said.

"You know I really never cared before I had the girls, and besides that, I did have a good childhood. I never wanted for anything. I think my adoptive mother and father were the best," Harmony said.

"How ironic it is that there were often times I wished I was adopted growing up with Bea, but I guess she did the best she could do, given the hand she had been dealt. Here you were adopted and would like to know your real parents. Well, all I can say is I support you all the way, girl, and just like anything else we've ever gone through, we'll get through this. We've gotten through much worst. Oooo, look at the time. I'd better get going. I have a full day tomorrow. I'll give you a call this weekend. Maybe we can drive to Woodfield to do some shopping and eating too, I hope. You know, I'm all for that. Let me know if there's anything I can do for you. By the way, thanks as usual for listening to me vent about my drama, and go easy on your baby girl. Tia will be alright. See you on Saturday. Let's plan to leave early."

"Alright. See you, girl, but one more thing, please promise me you will talk to Shea. The last thing you want to do is lose your baby girl right now. Like you said, society will make it hard enough for her. What you need to do is learn all you can about the lifestyle...hell, it's not a disease, and it's not uncommon. Ask yourself what bothers you so much about it...that's all I'mma say for now," Harmony said.

Bria thought about something she had heard on the Michael Baisden radio talk show: "A woman can raise a son but she can't teach him how to be a man." Lately, Bria had been hearing a lot of random dialogue by various African-American television talk show hosts and radio disc jockeys on radio talk shows and all of it seemed to have gotten on her nerves. It wasn't enough that she was constantly wondering what she could have done differently while raising her three children, but all the talk of how it should have been done and folks on the radio and television acting like they had all the answers to the problems was simply nerve wracking—or she wondered am I getting hit where it hurts.

"Some of those damn folks got to be lying," Bria said to her daughter India, commenting one morning after listening to one of her favorite commentators about something she had just heard on their radio talk show.

"Yeah, Mom, sometimes that stuff gets on my nerves too. Some of the talk I hear is like they're women bashing. A lot of times the topics that are discussed, I just want to call in and say something, then I think what's the use," India replied.

"*Umm-hmm.* I know what you mean. So do I," Bria answered.

Nonetheless, something must have been said that made Bria think, because lately there had been the constant thought of how she could have been a better parent. Not that Bria was obsessed—or maybe she was—but there was this burning passion to just have mentally healthy "normal" children. The focus now was to improve her life, and hopefully, her children would emulate her path. The children were self-sufficient—no longer were they babies in diapers. She was thinking things over and considering her youngest child. Shea had one more year in high school, and Bria surmised it was never too late for improvement.

"I can't go back and undo things now. Life hasn't been a bed of roses for me either, but I made the best of it. I just want these kids to know that anything is possible and for them not to let the unfortunate circumstances in life whatever it comes from—be it bad parenting, bad choices that they themselves make or fate itself—to not let any of those things be used as a crutch to not want to do better."

Chapter Eight

OVER THE YEARS, BRIA HAD remained close friends with Lynette from back in the day. It was Lynette and her husband Dale who had introduced Bria to Rad. Lynette had phoned to say she was throwing a surprise birthday party for Dale's fortieth birthday. It had taken all night for her to find the perfect get-up as India would always say when describing the perfect outfit to wear for any event. Since receiving the invitation, Bria had been indecisive about going to the party. She was thinking it could have been a setup and that Rad might be there. It was India who convinced her that perhaps she should attend.

"Mom, you need to get out. Don't you get tired of sitting around this house all the time?" asked India who was now twenty-two.

"Honey, the only thing I'm tired of is working and coming home and finding your behind on my phone," she responded halfheartedly.

"Whatever, Mom. You need to get out and have some fun, girl," India quirked. "Oh yeah, Lynette called. She said to bring the potato salad with you when you come. She said it'd be fine."

"Shit. I almost forgot about that part of the damn party. I did tell girlfriend I would make that potato salad. Damn."

"Duh, you know you always make the potato salad, Mom. Who else's potato salad would they want?"

"*Hmmph.* With all these damn Walmarts around here, anybody can buy potato salad," Bria snapped.

"Well, I guess they don't want anybody's or no dang Walmart potato salad. They want Bria Hudson's potato salad," India said.

"Yeah, okay. Now get off my phone, I need to call Lynette," she demanded.

She retreated to her spacious bedroom to confirm the details of the evening. She attempted to de-stress from the day at the office and wondered what would happen next.

"Let's see...what shall I to wear to this gala affair?" she said sarcastically while she searched for choices through the crammed closet.

Bria loved her friend Lynette, but she had often thought Lynette went overboard doing things for Dale. Bria and most of their close circle knew first-hand that Dale cheated on Lynette. They knew because Dale didn't try to hide it. Bria had learned from previous experience not to tell a friend when her man was cheating, so she thought it best not to tell Lynette about Dale.

One reason was she had been in a similar ordeal in the past, and that friend didn't take the news so well. It got so bad that her previous friend accused her of being jealous of her relationship. That friend and her boyfriend stayed together while she and Bria lost friendship. From that point on, Bria vowed to not interfere with her friends' relationships unless it was life or death.

But that didn't keep Bria from privately thinking Lynette was acting foolish over Dale. Bria would never tell her though. She loved Lynette and did not want to lose their friendship. Bria knew Lynette had to see for herself, so she planned to be there for Lynette when that time came.

She laughed to herself as she thought about all the things she had gone through with Rad. She thought it was funny how she looked at someone else's situation and was so quick to analyze what they should or should not do.

She walked over to the adjoining bathroom to run her bath, lit a candle and poured a fragrance of jasmine and shea butter bath soufflé into the hot running water. The soothing smells relaxed Bria. She allowed the aromatherapy to fill her nostrils and began her metamorphosis into luxurious passion. Now all that was missing was the sweet sounds of Maze's "Golden Time of Day," which sounded good any time of the day. She clicked on the sound system, but "The Morning After" chimed on. She loved the smooth sounds of Frankie Beverly and Maze.

She pretended she was dancing with a tall, dark, handsome man. She began to float across the floor, gliding like her man was leading her across the dance floor. Turns and dips, she was dancing, pretending Frankie was present and singing to her. She wondered what it would be like to have a man be to her what Frankie sang like and about. He was so smooth—so, so smooth. She let herself go, getting caught up in the words detailing a scenario of a man and woman in a relationship. The words were something about how they would feel the next morning as it related to having spent an evening being intimate.

Bria loved hearing the vocals of Frankie Beverly and believed that man was something else. She was a hopeless romantic. It seemed clichéd, but she wanted someone to serenade her and treat her like what Frankie sang about in his music. She wanted someone to want her in the worst kind of way. She wondered if she was too much of a dreamer. Perhaps she was. She had to snap out of it.

Bria loved the contralto voice of Anita Baker equally as much she loved hearing Frankie Beverly and Lisa Stansfield. In her opinion, those artists were her favorites and offered real music. It seemed no matter how often she heard her favorites—"Happy Feeling," "The Golden Time of Day," "Rapture," "Sweet Love," "All Around The World," "You Can't Deny It"—the songs never grew tiresome as far as she was concerned.

Then there was the spirit-filled vocals of Vanessa Bell Armstrong and Donnie McClurkin, which gave Bria the strength to endure the divorce. Music filled her mental psyche and was part of the healing therapy used to escape her daily stresses. Some folks exercised or chopped wood and some would choose to overeat, but Bria's passion was music and surrounding herself with beautiful things in her home.

The bath was a ritual she had afforded herself at least once a weekend since during the weekdays she mostly took showers. It was the one occasion during the day she allowed herself to be free to get in touch with her inner self—a moment to pamper and know herself. Sometimes she would just drift into faraway places—places of complete freedom and serenity. The routine would be condensed tonight; no time for the usual long bath she was accustomed to for the night was well spent. She had promised Lynette she would bring potato salad for Dale's surprise party.

"This is cute." She pulled out a lime green jersey tank, along with a flowing floral skirt. "Now where's that piece I got from It Boutique?" She fingered each satin hanger searching for the green tie-dyed silk poncho.

She always wore clothes that complemented her figure.

"Just 'cause I'm full figured doesn't mean I want to dress like an elastic waist, square jacket bama mama," she would say to India while on shopping sprees.

Bria Hudson made it a point to purchase clothes that enhanced her figure, always keeping in mind a saying she heard from Oprah: Just because it's in your size doesn't mean it's your size. Physically, Bria was described as having a pear shape, so she liked to wear clothes that enhanced her body style, and typically, she completed her look for any occasion quite well.

Bria had always received compliments on her legs, so she typically wore dresses along with stilettos that enhanced her overall appearance. Most of her friends admired her style and taste in clothing. She had to admit she enjoyed fashionable clothing and shoes, and even as a child watching Bea get dressed for the club and church she always liked getting dressed up in nice stuff. In some ways she thought the clothing covered the scars from her past and made her feel confident and secure even though there were times she wanted to curl up and die. Bria took one more glance in the floor-length mirror behind the door and liked her reflection. Her outfit matched her mood for the evening—fun and free-spirited comfort. The sandals were feminine and complemented her legs and her French pedicure completed the look. She was set to go.

It took about twenty minutes for Bria to drive to Lynette's. Plenty of alone space to reflect and meditate. It was usually during those periods when she would think of Shea. Bria kept telling herself she was to blame for what Shea was going through. In her mind, she felt she was a bad mother.

"You know some women just aren't cut out to be mothers," she had thought once and said openly to her other good friend Harmony. Sounds crazy, she would think, one can't pick and choose one's relatives. She knew deep inside what she was thinking and feeling was not right. While she had grown since the divorce, there were still issues that needed to be dealt with. She would find life simply just was not that easy. Life was complicated. There would be obstacles along the way. Things would occur that would catch one off guard when least expected. Blame was a still a big issue for her when it came to her children.

Lately, what she mostly thought about and found somewhat amusing was the fact that her baby was gay. How could this be? Bria tried so hard to deal with these circumstances but was having a very difficult time with the situation. Why? she kept asking herself. Why?

The party turned out well. Lynette had about thirty guests.

The evening started at about eight-ish and lasted until about midnight. The big hit of the night was Lynette's guests doing an urban dance commonly known as Steppin' that originated out of Chicago.

Lynette also had music jamming to the sounds of Loose Ends, Luther Vandross, Chaka Khan, Miki Howard, and Freddie Jackson, and Lynette had polished her hardwood floors in an adjoining living room and dining room area spacious enough for plenty of stepping and dipping. She had transformed her living quarters into an ole school night of birthday fun and dance.

"Girl, I am getting too old for this," Bria said to Lynette as she was ending a dance and reaching for a glass of lemon water.

"Remember what your momma used to tell us? Don't nothin' get old but clothes," Lynette said.

"Okay, I'll try to remember that when I get my tired ass up tomorrow or when my legs are aching from all this stepping I'm doing tonight," Bria said.

"You'll be alright, girl. Now get on back out there and keep stepping the night away," Lynette said.

On the drive home Bria thought about how much fun she'd had. She needed to clear her head and get her mind off Shea for a while. It had been a while since she got out for a night of fun and dancing with so much on her mind. She was exhausted from all the dancing and looked forward to bed when she got home since she had been having trouble sleeping. It was around ten the next morning when she decided to move around.

"Stayed out kinda late last night, didn't you, girl?" India teased her mother.

"Twelve o'clock is not late," she responded.

"It's late for you, Mom. You're usually in bed by ten. So did you have a good time?" India asked, sitting on the edge of Bria's bed.

"Yeah, I have to admit I did for a change. Danced my butt off, I know that."

"Oh my God, I'll bet you did," India remarked.

"Girl, you can say what you want. I know I can dance. Ooo, what time is it? Let me get up and get a move on. Make sure Shea is up. How about breakfast?" Bria asked.

"Sounds fine to me. You buying or are you cooking?" India asked.

"It would be nice if you tried to cook an egg or something, India," Bria said, shuffling the feathered comforter.

"In time, mother dear, I will. Oh, and by the way, did you tell Shea she could spend the night at Monique's last night? 'Cause that's what she said, and she's not home."

"What? Well, Shea lied. She told me Monique was spending the night here with her. I think she's pulled a fast one. Give me the phone."

She could feel the tensing in her head as she dialed the number to Monique Slay's home. Monique and Shea had been friends since second grade, and the two girls had been inseparable ever since. Bria didn't know what to expect as she phoned the Slays' residence. The phone had been ringing for at least ten seconds with no one answering. Bria then dialed Shea's cell phone number.

"Yelllo. Ha. Thought you had me. Speak at the beep and leave a message."

Irritated by the phone message, Bria ended the call.

"I know she knows I'm trying to call her. She'd better get her butt here, I know that."

She felt things had been so complicated lately with Shea. Bria wondered what Shea was thinking and what made her misbehave so much. She had noticed a change in Shea's temperament and had scheduled a counseling session, but once she and her daughter arrived at the appointment, Shea made such a mockery of the event that Bria didn't bother to take her to see the counselor again. That was another regret she had. She never seemed to finish what she started. She had benefited from the co-dependency counseling sessions that she attended while Rad was in drug abuse treatment and thought the children would benefit as well. However, when asked, they all refused.

She thought things couldn't get any worse than her own dysfunctional childhood. Reminiscing about the times with Bea were enough to make her feel counseling was definitely in order. At least for her it was. There was the time she remembered having to literally fight for her life from her mother.

She had never shared with anyone the story about when she once had to defend herself from one of her mother's bouts of alcoholic rages. Bea would try to fight her when she believed there were people in the house. Knowing more about alcoholism and its effect on the family, she now knew her mother was hallucinating, but she didn't know it then. There was one time when she wished she was dead or adopted. She couldn't believe the way her mother came at her. Bria recalled incidents where she would be afraid to sleep at night for fear Bea would come into her room and attack her. One night during a below-zero-temperature evening, she had to run to the neighbor's house barefoot and clad only in a nightgown because Bea was coming at her with a knife threatening to kill her. To this day, she wondered how she made it out of that situation. She was glad those moments were over. That was one of the many dark secrets she would share with no one for fear she would be judged as a bad girl or not good enough.

In spite of all those bad scenarios in her life, her mother was the most important person she loved. There seemed to be two personalities—the sober, loving, and nurturing mother and the alcoholic abusive side to Bea. Only time would heal the pain Bria faced as a child growing up.

Chapter Nine

BRIA WATCHED FROM THE FRONT window as the small Ford she had purchased for her daughter Shea rolled into her drive-way. The wheels stopped, and she watched as Shea got out the driver's side of the vehicle and started to walk to the side of the house.

Bria could feel the tension brewing inside her as she waited impatiently for her daughter to enter the house.

"Shea, I thought you said Monique was staying the night here with you. Where have you been? I'll tell you what, give me those car keys and that cell phone. You're grounded until I say other-wise. Since you're trying to act like you're grown and disre-specting my rules to be home when I tell you then no more freedom to use my transportation or my cell phone. Those things are privileges that I provide to you, but you have abused them. You think you can just waltz in here as you please and do whatever it is you feel like doing. Let me tell you, it don't work that way. Unless you get my permission first, you don't get privileges. I demand respect and need to know where you're going before you go. You don't get to just do your own thing—not in this house. The problem is, I've made things way too easy for you. You've proven over and over that you have no respect for authority, but you're going to learn. I won't tolerate this behavior. I don't understand how you can be such a liar."

"Mom, what are you talking about? You haven't given me a chance to say anything. I told you before you left last night that Monique was staying over here *or* I would be staying the night at her house, and you say it was okay...dang, at the time, we really hadn't decided on which house we would stay at. Why are you making such a big deal out of it?" Shea said.

"Shea, if you were at Monique's, why is it that you failed to call home? You have a cell phone. You could have called as soon as the plan changed. That's the purpose of you having a phone, so I can reach you and you can let me know your whereabouts. I know you're lying because I tried to call you, but you didn't answer. You think I don't know why that is? It's because you don't want to be found. You want to be somewhere doing Lord knows what with Lord knows who. I truly don't understand you, girl. You say one thing and do another. I may not ever understand this mess, but I tell you one thing, I'm not aiding and abetting you in this foolishness. Get out of my face before I say something I might regret," Bria said.

Shea walked out of the room.

I'm really struggling with this thing with Shea. What the hell do I do with this? How do I deal with this? What is the message, Lord? What really is the message? I know you said weeping may endure for a night, but Lord, how long is the night? I know everything happens for a reason. What is the reason I'm going through this? And why do I have a child that on one hand is more caring than the average nun and on the other hand lies more than the common thief? I literally don't know how to reach this child. Lord, please help me understand what's going on with her before I lose my baby.

Bria was having a typical Saturday afternoon. The morning started out cleaning house, burning candles, doing laundry, and opening windows. The breeze from the opened windows was very comforting. The sweet, succulent smell of the Grand Canyon lilac–scented candle permeated the air in subtle wisps. She decided to take a ride out to T.J. Maxx, then swing over to the Burlington Coat Factory before she headed over to Bea's apartment.

When she pulled up to the four-family apartment dwelling, she immediately saw one of Bea's neighbors, seventy-nine-year-old Mister Ray standing on the sidewalk. Bria thought, *Damn. I hate coming over here. I sure as hell don't feel like being bothered with Mister Ray today.*

Mister Ray typically hung around outside the apartments. It was the neighborhood rumor that Mister Ray's forty-something-year-old lady friend lived in the apartment with him, but she was using him for his money, a place to live, and weed. The gossips said she only showed up around the first of the month when Mister Ray received his Social Security benefits. Mister Ray was hunched over and was usually shabbily dressed and rarely shaved. Bria despised seeing him because of the way he stared at her breasts and watched her butt when he spoke to her. Often when he looked at a woman, it seemed as if he had x-ray vision. He didn't just admire a woman. His stare seemed to pierce the very core of who he chose as his target as if he was trying to see beneath the woman's clothing. Bria felt so uneasy around him.

"Hi, baby," Mister Ray said.

"Hi, Mister Ray. How are you today?" Bria replied, not missing a beat in her stride as she proceeded up the sidewalk to her mother's apartment door. She was always cordial to Mister Ray but didn't waste a lot of time waiting for a reply from him or inviting any additional small talk.

Bria never knew what to expect from Bea. On any given day, Bea was in rare form. Today was no different. Bea was in her usual character.

"Come on in here," Bea said, waving.

Bria could see by the looks of the place and Bea's appearance that her mother had been drinking, but she tried to overlook it and act polite. "Hey Beaddie. Whatcha doing in here, sweetie?"

Lately, even in lieu of the drinking, she had been noticing a slight change in Bea's behavior. There would be short periods of time that lasted as long as two weeks in which Bea would take a break from the alcohol. Bria figured it could have been because she was sick or she lacked funds to get the brand she wanted, or it could have been that she simply grew tired of how it made her feel. Whatever the reason, Bria didn't know or understand why she couldn't just quit altogether. Bria liked her personality when she wasn't under the influence, and they got along much better, but she loved her either way. When Bea wasn't inebriated, her apartment was clean, smelled fresh, and she cooked. This wasn't one of those times. The house wasn't clean. There were sections of newspaper on the narrow hallway floor, and a strong peculiar odor met Bria's nostrils. It smelled like something had spoiled. She stooped to gather the newspapers from the floor leading to the kitchen of the small apartment. The smell over-whelmed her as she got closer to the area. Sitting in the sink was a red pail of thawed pork intestines.

"Beaddie, how long have you had these chitlins in this sink?" Bria asked.

"I'm cleaning these for Benny. He brought them over yester-day," Bea said.

"*Hmmph.* You sure they're alright? I don't think Benny's gon-na want these thangs. It's pretty warm in here. I could smell them as soon as I walked up to your door. I don't think Benny should mess with this. You know what, I'll take these to my house and finish cleaning them up for you and take them to Benny. How about that? That way you don't have to mess with them," Bria said.

"Shit. He paid me ten dollars to clean 'em. I got drunk. I did-n't feel like cleaning no damn chitlins. Aww what the hell. It's alright."

Bea threw up her hands and started popping her fingers and swaying her body, dancing to the music in her head. Bria watched her mother's performance. Bea stood and started gy-rating and twisting to sounds that only she heard. Bria proceed-ed to clean up the sink. She gathered up the newspapers off the floor, stuffed the papers in the bottom of a trash bag, and put the chitterlings in the bag. She knew her mother would oppose her throwing any food out, so she acted like she was going to take the pail home with her, knowing she would put them in the trash.

She spent a while going from room to room to ensure the small apartment was tidied up before returning to the kitchen to complete the finishing touches. She looked under the sink to obtain a bottle of Lysol disinfectant spray to deodorize. Sitting next to the Lysol was a gallon bottle of Canadian Club whiskey half empty. She ignored the bottle and got the Lysol. After so many years of finding empty whiskey bottles, she had learned to let her mother be. Time had made it easier to deal with her mother's drinking, especially since she was an adult and didn't have to live with her anymore.

"Well, I guess that does it, " Bria said.

Bea was oblivious to her daughter's cleaning around the apartment and kept on with her own thing. Bria was used to her mother's behavior when she was under the influence, so she didn't let it bother her and continued with the cleaning. Then she thought she had better inspect the refrigerator since Bea had a bad habit of leaving spoiled food in it for long periods.

One of her pet peeves was when Bea would put a bowl of something in the refrigerator with a stainless steel spoon or fork left in the food. Bria thought she had heard that was unsanitary and could cause poisoning, so she would always check to be sure her mother wasn't eating any bad food or that there wasn't any old food in the refrigerator. She always tried to make sure the apartment was neat even though she knew as soon as she left, things got out of order again. At least she felt comfort in knowing she tried to see to it that her mother's surroundings were pretty decent.

"Love you, darling. I don't let small things like cleaning up bother me. What do you want? You need anything, baby? Pass my purse. I have something. I'm not broke," Bea said.

It was never uncommon for Bea to offer Bria something when she visited—food, money, anything. Bria couldn't figure out why she did that and thought perhaps that was her motherly nature kicking in.

"Beaddie, I don't need anything. I just stopped by to check on you. Did you take your medicine today?" Bria asked.

"I'm fine, darling. You don't have to worry about me."

"Did you eat today? What did you have for dinner?"

"Yes, of course, darling. I got food. I ate," Bea said.

She wondered how Bea could have taken any medicine when she had been drinking, and judging from that bottle under the sink, she had been drinking quite a bit. She knew her mother was on prescription drug medicine for high blood pressure among other things and wondered how she had maintained her health and functioned as well as she did. Bria couldn't remember a time in her life that Bea didn't drink, but nothing seemed to stop her—not the health issues, the events spent in the hospital, several times in their past, Bria wondered how she was still living with all the close calls she had.

Back when Bria was sixteen, she could remember being at a doctor's appointment with Bea, and the physician refused to see Bea because she wouldn't follow his instructions. Bria tried to shake that memory. Just thinking about it brought about a wave of embarrassment all over again. Bria could not figure out what Bea could have been thinking by making a teenager attempt to schedule an appointment.

Bria had no choice but to do as her mother instructed. Not knowing what the outcome would be, Bria went to the desk and told the receptionist why she was there, but to her shock and horror, the receptionist succinctly and emphatically requested she leave and to let her mother know not to come back per the doctor's request. She would never forget the humiliation she felt from that experience. She knew Bea had been under that particular doctor's care for quite some time, so she found it difficult to process yet comprehend the reason for his actions.

During holidays, birthdays and other special events, Bria would reminisce and spend time thinking about some of the memorable occasions she spent with her closest friends and their families. Bria had developed the habit of constant fantasy. She often spent hours daydreaming about how she believed her life should be. She constantly compared her experiences to that of most of her closest friends.

As a child, Bria spent a lot of time with friends and their families. Bria was grateful and was glad. She always looked forward to the holidays such as Thanksgiving, Christmas, Easter, and the Fourth of July because she got invited out and didn't have to be alone with Bea.

Bria secretly fantasized about being adopted by one of her friends' parents because they seemed to treat her like one of their own children. It was a fantasy she embodied that never materialized. Instead, Bria dealt with reality as she knew it and longed for the day a change would come.

Bria loved Bea in her own way, and despite everything they had been through, she felt an obligation and loyalty to be there for her. As far as immediate family was concerned, in Rockford, Bea was the most significant person to Bria and the children. Bea had been there for them in the past and picked up the slack when Bria endured financial hardships due to having to provide for her and the kids due to broken relationships.

Bria made whatever sacrifices she could to make sure her children's basic needs were met but still struggled providing food and paying bills. So Bea would provide whatever she had to give—whether it was a frozen chicken, a loaf of bread, a bag of potatoes, Bea always made sure Bria and the children had what they needed. Bea didn't have that much to give, but she made sacrifices and provided money for bills even when Bria had a husband. It was Bea who had supported Bria and the children.

By the time Bria left the apartment, Bea had grown tired, and Bria had convinced her to get dressed for bed, then locked up and left. Bria sort of laughed to herself as the thought crossed her mind that no amount of self-help books in the world could ever understand her personal story. She wondered if anyone could ever imagine what she'd gone through.

Chapter Ten

BRIA COULDN'T WAIT TO GET home after her visit with Bea so she could retreat to her bath. Often the visits with Bea left her feeling emotionally drained. Soaking in a hot drawn tub of water with soothing aromatherapy fragrances met her insatiable desire for comfort and solace.

The bath was more soothing than anticipated. She sank deeper into the hot sudsy water and surrendered to its calmness. She usually found peace and tranquility when bathing, and for some reason was able to accept things she had no control over and sort out to deal with situations as they were.

After drying the suds from her curvaceous caramel skin, she rubbed lotion on her body, put on a gown then climbed into bed, said a quiet prayer and drifted off to sleep for the night.

When morning came, Bria awakened to the radio alarm.

"Whew. I must have been tired." She hit the off button and sunk back on the pillow before getting out of bed. "I better get my butt up before I oversleep. I'd better have that dreaded conversation with Shea today to find out what's going on with her. I've put that off long enough...mental note to self, first thing after work...sit down with Shea."

On her way out the house that morning, Bria had stopped by Shea's room to let her know to be home so they could talk when she got in.

Later that evening, Bria got home around five thirty as expected on any other regular day. As Bria pulled in to the driveway, she started to feel a certain sense of anxiety build up as she thought about what she would say to her daughter or better yet the unknown Shea might say to her. Just like most things in life that made her uneasy, Bria had hoped she was making more out of what she heard Shea discussing on the phone than what it was and that it would ultimately work itself out instead of having to confront the matter. She realized what she'd overheard Shea talking about with whomever she was speaking was not something she could pretend she hadn't heard. Bria had to talk to Shea and understand it.

The house seemed unusually quiet as Bria entered the entrance from the garage to the famliy room, which led to the kitchen. She looked on the kitchen counter to see if any mail was there, then headed back to her room to place her things and looked up the stairs and wondered whether Zach, India or Shea were home. She had hoped no one was other than Shea.

"Shea, you home? Come on down," Bria yelled.

"Hey, Mom, I uh don't know how to tell you, but Shea's not here," India said from the top of the staircase.

"What? What do you mean she's not here?" Bria asked.

"I'm not trying to be disrespectful, Mom, but what part of she's not here didn't you hear? She's not here. Maybe she's running late, but clearly she's not here yet," India said.

"You are being very disrespectful, India, and you better watch yourself, little girl. You're crossing the line. Really? *Hmmph.* She was to be here by the time I got home so we could talk," Bria said.

"Well, I hate to be the one to tell you this, but the other night when you confronted her about Monique, she came in my room cussing and saying how you never listen to her, and you knew she might spend the night over to Monique's. She said all you do is—'cuse me for cussing, but she said, all you do is—bitch, bitch, bitch. She said a lot more, but I would rather not repeat it. Mom, I think you need to talk to her—and fast. Something isn't right with her. Have you noticed how she's been acting lately?" India asked.

"Well, there are some things I know I need to talk with her about, and that's what I had planned to do today," Bria said.

"Yeah, that's a good idea, and Mom, I know you like to make your point sometimes by yelling and cussing, but this time you might try a different approach with Shea. You need to fix this before it gets worse," India said.

"Girl, what are you talking about? Do you know something you're not telling me? What do you mean fix? Fix what? How the hell can I fix something when I don't know what's broken? Anyhow, I'm not some grand wizard who can go around fixing stuff and situations you guys get yourselves in. What is going on? Will somebody please tell me?" Bria said.

"There you go, mother dear. Try not to work yourself up. I'm just saying. Uh-oh, look who just walked in. Saved by the bell," India said, seeing Shea walk in.

"Hey, Mom. Sorry, I'm late," Shea said.

"Whatever, but you had me worried. I thought you might not have been here on purpose. Sit down. We need to talk. What's going on with you? Is there anything you want to discuss with me, something I need to know—anything?" Bria asked.

"No, not really. You just don't listen to me, and like I told you the other night, I asked you about going over to Monique's, and you said it was okay, then I said we might stay over here. But what happened was I drove to her house and parked my car. Monique's mom agreed to take us to the game and pick us up so we didn't have to worry about parking. So when her mom picked us up from the game, she really didn't want to bring me home, so I told her you said it was okay for me to stay over there," Shea said.

"Okay. I don't want to keep going over that. If that's the case, then it must have really slipped my mind because I don't recall those details. Sounds like a farfetched lie to me. You are going to try and make me believe Monique's mother agreed to all that when you could have driven yourself. Whatever...what I want to talk to you about has to do with a conversation I overheard you discussing on the phone a few nights ago. Sounded like you were talking with someone about kissing and you doing her next time. I don't know what that was implying, but it did not sound good to me, and it sounded like it was a girl you were talking with because I heard you call a girl's name during the conversation. Let me just ask 'cause right now I don't know any other way than to lay it out on the line with you. Are you gay?"

"Naww! What are you talking about?" Shea asked.

"Look, don't lie to me. I know what I heard. It sounded like you were talking to a girl. You said something to the effect of her kissing you and next time you will kiss her, but that right now you aren't ready. I'm asking you to tell me the truth. What's going on? Is someone making you do something against your will? Please tell me the truth," Bria said.

"Mom, I know how you are. If I tell you the truth about something you don't like, you always go off. You promise not to go over to anyone's house going off? I know you. You always go off about stuff," Shea said.

"Just tell me what's going on, I hope it's not that bad to where I'll need to go off as you put it. Just say it. Tell me, please. Whatever it is, I want to know—I need to know," Bria said.

"Well, I have a new friend. Her name is Chelsea Robinson. She's a nice girl. We met at the basketball tryouts. You would like her too if you got to know her. The thing is you are always judging people," Shea said.

"This is not making sense to me, Shea. Are you telling me that Chelsea is your girlfriend or what?" Bria asked.

"No. Ain't nobody thinking about that. We're just friends," Shea said.

"Well, if that's the case, why haven't I met this Chelsea? And why have you kept her such a secret? I know all your friends and their parents, but this is the first time I've heard about

Chelsea," Bria said.

"If you want to meet her, you can. When do you want to? I can call her now. She doesn't live that far from us," Shea said.

"No, it's too short notice now, but tomorrow when I get home, she can come over then. I would like to meet her for myself. Let me say this: Something is still not clear to me. I know what I overheard, and you are not being upfront about it yet. Whether it be boy or girl, pre-marital sex is not something I'll condone. You have your whole life ahead of you. There are other things you need to be concerned about right now, so please don't allow anyone to force you into doing something you are not ready for or that you'll regret for the rest of your life. The other thing is all this sneaking out the house and lying has got to stop too. I need to know I can trust you. It's difficult for me to work and worry about what's going on at home. I'm asking for your cooperation. Please don't make it any harder for me than it already is. Do we have an understanding?" Bria said.

"Yeah, Mom, I get it. I've gotta go now. I have homework to do," Shea said.

"Sure. Now give me a hug. We'll talk again tomorrow, same time, only this time you'll have Chelsea will be with you, right?" Bria asked.

After their talk, Bria still wasn't convinced Shea was telling her the truth, and she wasn't at ease with what Shea said about Chelsea being her new friend. Since eavesdropping on the conversation, Bria had started paying more attention to Shea's behavior and style of dress. It had never bothered her that her daughter only wanted black gym shoes and boy-style socks before then. Now she began to wonder if she had been missing the signs all alone.

Chapter Eleven

AS BRIA MEDITATED ON HOW to handle the situation with Shea, she couldn't help but think about Rad.

I really need to give his ass a call about this. I sure would like to know what he would do, she thought.

Since they'd divorced, Bria had little to no contact with Rad because he was still using drugs and she didn't want to deal with him. Rad provided little to no financial child support to Bria as a result his inability to maintain employment, but he and Shea continued to have a very close relationship.

Despite all their differences, Bria understood Rad was still Shea's father and deserved to know what was going on with their daughter. Bria knew he didn't have much to give financially, but he gave what he had, which was love. So Bria chose not to interfere nor did she want to hold it over his head how much he did or did not do for Shea financially as she believed it was equally important for him to have a relationship with Shea. That was the one thing she gave Rad credit for since there were some men who seemed to be able to go about their business as if they had no obligation to their children emotionally or financially.

In some ways, Bria admired Shea and Rad's relationship. She liked the father-daughter bond they had. Rad and Shea had the type of relationship she had longed for with her own father as a child. Bria had come to realize how not having that relationship with her dad had impacted her life, so she didn't want Shea to have to deal with the same experience. Bria had no idea what she was going to say to Rad, but she knew she needed to let him know what her suspicions were about Shea. In some sort of way, she was hoping Rad could fix Shea.

The one thought Bria had was she did not want to do to her children what Bea had done to her. Bria could not grasp why some men acted like they didn't care about their children and how insecure this could make them feel as well as the long-term detrimental effects it had on the child's life. That was why it was difficult for her to understand why Bea had not shared any information about Lee or why he hadn't acknowledged her. Then one day, which to Bria seemed like out of the blue, during a visit with her mother, Bea said, "Theodis is not your father. Lee Cox is."

Bria was startled and muttered without thinking, "What is she talking about?"

Bria felt like she had been hit with a ton of bricks.

Bria had known of Lee Cox and his wife, Ellie Lou, from the church she grew up in. It had been the church their family belonged to back in the early days when Bea and Uncle Earl first came to Rockford. It was the church that Uncle Earl said had nicknamed Bria "the church baby" because as he put it, she was such an adorable baby that on any given Sunday Bea was one of the last to leave church because Bria had been cuddled during service and often handed from member to member to be held.

So for Bea to say Lee Cox was her father was unfathomable and unimaginable. Bria thought it was downright cruel for her to have said it.

But at that instant, a flood of memories invaded her mind. On several occasions, Bria had viewed old clippings and pictures of her from birth to a toddler adorned in what looked like some of the best dresses, frilled socks, and patent leather shoes during events that had occurred at the church. In some of the photos, she was held by a man she didn't recognize. At first, she thought the man looked familiar, but she had not realized it was Lee Cox. Confused and in denial, she didn't want to accept that Lee Cox was her birth father.

Bea, in one of her epiphany moments, finally disclosed the true story about Lee to her daughter, but Bria refused to accept it. Growing up, she would often wonder what life would have been like had she grown up in the fine home Lee and Ellie Lou shared. Often, an intoxicated Bea drove her by Lee and Ellie Lou's home to admire the Christmas decorations. Seeing the beautiful decorations made Bria feel deprived of a lifestyle she had yearned for all her life. She felt betrayed and humiliated, angry, and of course, ashamed because Bria wondered why Lee, if he was in fact her birth father, hadn't he rescued her from Bea and the life she'd had to endure.

Bria recalled times she barely had food to eat, or times Bea would be so drunk that she slept most of the day and left Bria to fend for herself. She felt abandoned and wondered why Lee hadn't acknowledged her as his child. She questioned also why Bea hadn't demanded child support or something for her. But when asked, Bea would reply that Lee was married and that she wasn't going to ask a married man to support her or her child. That reply always left Bria stunned and bewildered. She could never understand her mother's reasoning.

Bria could not understand why Bea had allowed years to go by before she started bringing up Lee Cox's name again. Bria saw it coming, but one day out of nowhere Bea said to her, "Here, I think you should read this. It's an article about your father. I've been keeping it for you over the years. It's time you have it."

Like so many other antics Bea pulled in the past, Bria didn't know what to make of her actions, whether it was guilt, out of spite, or genuine concern. All of a sudden Bria noticed Bea had been relentless about her knowing Lee was her father. Bria held on to the old yellowed newspaper clipping Bea had given her for days before deciding to read it. It was titled "Reflections by the Man of the Year Contest Winner Lee Cox." It was a story written by Lee detailing his aspirations during that time to attend college after high school but how life's twist of fate turned the tables and instead he went to World War II. She found the article intriguing and began to wonder what Lee's personality and demeanor were like.

Bria had to admit after reading and learning things about him from the story, it had piqued her interest so much that she felt a breakthrough and believed she had mustered up enough courage to pick up the phone and call him, but she allowed self-doubt and other insecurities to get in her way.

Days continued to pass as she went about the same cycle. She would get an urge to call him then would talk herself out of it. Mentally, she struggled with this decision over and over, but in the end she convinced herself otherwise. She kept that article in her nightstand drawer near her bed and reread it often, and as she read, she thought about how she had spent nearly four decades of her life believing the man in the article. Her father didn't want anything to do with her but she never reached out to him to ask why. For so long, Bria didn't think she cared one way or another and had been in denial about knowing her father. She thought it was insignificant and meant nothing to her to ever want to know anything about him. Bria knew she was only lying to herself, and the more she thought about it, she realized she needed to speak with him. It was a feeling that would not go away.

Bria hadn't thought the past feelings of inadequacy, low self-esteem, people pleasing, insecurities dealing with relationships, and trust could have had to do with her not having had that father-daughter bond in her life. So without giving it another thought, she picked up her phone and the phone book, looked up the number and dialed it.

Bria was thankful she hadn't had to deal with some of the things she'd witnessed some of her friends in their neighborhood who were raised by single mothers dealing with. She thought about a time one of her neighborhood friend's mom asked her if she knew what commodity peanut butter was. When Bria responded no, the lady teased her and said, "Bea got you living in a fantasy world." It was years later that Bria realized these women were on welfare and things like commodity peanut butter, box cheese, and silver cans without labels were signs the groceries were public welfare brand foods.

Bria didn't mock her friends for getting public assistance. One reason was she never thought anything was wrong with it because she didn't know anything about welfare or what the benefits were because Bea was too proud to get that type of assistance. Even during the times when it was just the two of them when Bea was struggling to make ends meet, she still would not budge. Bea was adamant about not getting public help. Bea took extra lengths to send Bria to a private Catholic school. Bria knew some single parents in those days would not have made the sacrifice to do that. She had attended some of the best private schools during her adolescent years. Most of the students who attended the same schools had both parents. When there was only one parent, especially a mother, it was usually because the father was deceased. Rarely during the late sixties and early seventies in her environment was it just a single-parent situation by choice. Perhaps, that's why she felt so out of place.

One time, she befriended an unusual-looking, light-skinned African-American girl who was naturally redheaded. Bria thought it was odd to see an African-American redhead but found she and the girl had a few things in common, so they became best friends. They both excelled in school, had the same taste in music and clothes, and would even talk about what they thought they would like in boys. When her friend led her to believe that if a child did not have both parents, the mother must have been a whore and the children were bastards, she felt ashamed because she knew her mother's situation. Looking back, she just shook her head at the thought of how she would try to fit in with so many people's lives. She wore so many faces that she literally did not know who she was or what she liked.

"Whew, thank you, Lord. I made it another day," Bria exclaimed as she put the key in the ignition of her vehicle.

Bria had just ended another day at the plant and was headed home. Simultaneously pulling the seat belt over her shoulder and fastening the clamp, she then turned on the radio and slowly accelerated out of the parking stall. Instead of music, she heard an advertisement: "Live your dreams, people. Money ain't everythang and pardon my vernacular. Hold on to your passion. Call in and let me know how many folks out there are living with a degree and hate your job."

"Here we go again: Live your dreams, live your passion. What bullshit," she said, listening to the radio jock. "Hell, if I could live my dreams, I sure in the hell wouldn't be at this damn place. These damn folks are wearing me down. I'm so sick of this bull 'til I don't know what to do. But Lord, don't get me wrong, you know I need my job, but I sure am tired of kissing ass at this damn place."

"People, listen, live your passion…" Bria tuned out the radio jock.

"Okay, Mr. D.J., all of you just happened to be in the right place at the right time. I don't believe none of what you all say. Lord, what is my passion? Show me what I'm supposed to be doing. I know it's got to be more than this."

Bria worked twenty miles south of Rockford, out in rural Pine Grove, Illinois. The town had prospered since the construction of the power plant. Pine Grove had become quite an elite town. Pine Grove High, a state-of-the-art high school, had a heated indoor track the size of two football stadiums. There were surrounding subdivisions with houses worth $175,000 to $250,000 afforded by mostly the senior management of the plant. The remaining lower management and some bargaining union employees lived in neighborhoods with market homes ranging from $90,000 to $120,000.

The town was predominantly white farmers and car dealership owners. Commonly farmers' spouses sought jobs at the plant for insurance purposes. Many individuals didn't like the size. They thought the city was too large, the school system was bad, and felt the crime rate was too high, so they didn't want their children exposed to any of that and preferred to live in the rural areas outside of Rockford.

Bria tried to understand why some of her white counterparts thought they could get away with being unfair on occasion, but she couldn't rationalize it other than to figure it had to do with the demographics and cultural upbringing. After attending the funeral of one of her white colleagues, it became evident to her that most of them had literally no experience at all of dealing with people of color as was indicative she and a black male co-worker were the only African-Americans in attendance. Bria felt like she was in the twilight zone because of some of the looks they got.

Like Bria, the few African-Americans who worked at the

plant commuted from Rockford to the rural area where the plant was located. Most of the white employees lived in the vicinity. Twelve out of 740 employees were African-American. So sad in her opinion to have to deal with some of what they had to endure just to earn a decent living. One thing Bria knew for sure was her time at the company afforded her an opportunity to provide nice things for her family. Even still, she was tired of always feeling like she had to prove herself in the workplace.

Bria had always been taught to work hard and to do her best, and she tried to instill that same work ethic in her children. Even though she was grateful to be of the one percent African-American number in the workplace, she couldn't help but to second guess why she remained in such a toxic environment. She mentally questioned over and over whether it was need or greed, whether the material benefits outweighed the frustration of dealing with some of the narrowmindedness that went on at the plant. To that end, Bria knew one day she would have to make some changes to be happy and fulfilled. She was tired of thinking about it. She needed to do something about it.

After getting settled at home later in the evening, Bria phoned her friend Harmony just to catch up and chat.

"I just feel like I'm drowning, Harm, and drowning fast," Bria said.

"Okay. Pull yourself together, Bria. Where's your faith? You know things will get better," Harmony said.

"Harm, I think I need a change. You ask me where's my faith? That's just it, I do have faith. I have faith that I know I'll be alright if I just follow my heart and do what I love. I believe in time I'll be alright. Girlfriend, do you know how difficult it is coming to that plant every day, working to please folks who no matter what I do, there's no pleasing them? I'm ready to start living on my own terms. I believe I'm productive. I put in the long hours, and still, what have I got to show for it? I'm completely miserable there. I'm serious. I'm considering putting in my resignation," Bria said.

"Bria, you've been at the plant twenty years. What about your family, your retirement, your pension?"

"What about it? I'm forty-seven years old; I'm not getting any younger. Look around me. My children are all grown up. Zach has moved out and is working and paying his own way through college. India is working and attending community college. Eventually she needs to consider getting her own place. She thinks I don't know it, but she spends the night with that boyfriend of hers so much that she might as well move in with him. But whatever, that's her choice. I don't have to live with them.

"Harm, I've cared for other folks in my life since I was sixteen. When have I ever made a decision lately solely based on my happiness and what I want? You can't answer that because for over forty-plus years, all I've done is made decisions based on what was best for my mom, best for my kids, best for my marriage. It's time for me. Like I said, I'm in my late forties. What if God doesn't give me another forty-something more years? I'll have lived my entire life based on other folks' feelings and not my own. I feel it. I've got to make some changes, and this time the changes I make will be for me," Bria said.

"Okay, girlfriend. Sounds like you've been putting some thought into this. Have you given this much consideration—I mean some serious meditation? I know how you like to write things down, always weighing your pros and cons. Have you written down the pros and cons yet?" Harmony asked.

"Yes, I have. I've jotted down a few things, and guess what, Harm. I've been so bogged down lately all I know is something must give. Every time I go to that plant and walk to the far end of what seems like nowhere to what they call my office, I just want to puke. I can feel it in my gut, I know it's time for me to make a change," Bria said.

"If you're sure, I have your back. So tell me what your plans are," Harmony said.

"Well, to be honest, I've given this much thought. I have a pretty good 401(k) plan and our company is one of few places that offers a pension as well. So with that being said, I think I'm going to resign, retire, whatever. I can use some of the money from my 401(k) to get me started so I should be okay until I figure out what my next move will be. But what I know for sure is I'm not happy where I am," Bria said.

"Sounds a little risky to me, especially coming from you. You've always been so safe and logical, Bri," Harmony asked.

"I know, but what's life without any risks? I don't know what the future holds, but I know I'll regret it if I don't try to do something different. I just feel now is the time. For quite some time, I've been journaling to clear my head. That's a good thing, you know. When you journal, it helps to put things in perspective. Often, you can go back and see where you are in life and learn from those times. I've discovered I can see things from a different perspective then. Some of my stuff I've gone back and read is quite interesting if I must say so myself. I've even found some of it pretty amusing. I don't know where I'm headed yet. I'm getting to know myself better. Like I said, occasionally I'll go back and read some of my passages to see where my head was during certain periods, and it helps me to see how far I've come or if I'm still stuck at the same place. You'd be surprised to see your own growth and even how stupid some of it I, I'm just saying. Some of what I wrote is so painfully stupid and..." Bria realized she couldn't go on, so she just ended and said, "Oh well, it is what it is. I just take it as that and move on."

"Well, I know one damn thing for sho. We sure as hell got some shit to write about. Somebody ought to make some money off some of this shit," Harmony said.

They both laughed.

"So, back to what I was saying, I don't plan to quit my day job tomorrow, but I think I do have a good transition plan—in two years, I'm out of there. Harm, that damn power plant isn't the only thing I know how to do, and lately, I know the more I sit in those meetings, the less I care about tasks related to incident reporting and tracking actions, qualification management, or any other power politicking bullshit. That's all it is to me is bullshit.

"Don't get me wrong, I have nothing against the power plant industry. It's a great thing. Some of the folks running it are some geniuses; some of them running it are some jerks too. Regardless, I don't fit in that world—it's not my personality. That's all I'm saying. While I'm there though, I'll put my time in and do my job, and I plan to perform to the highest level of professionalism. It's just that sometimes I can't overlook all that's going on in that place. It's just that racism that I'm sick of, and believe it or not, most of it's not subtle at all. It's blatant—right in your face stuff. Yeah, I know racism exists all over and will be forever until the day we die, and I know you get tired of my ranting and complaining about it, but I am soooo sick of it. If it weren't for the fact the pay was so good, I woulda been gone. I'll at least be doing something I'm passionate about. I wish I had the power to believe in me.

"I'll betcha this: My next go-round, I won't be working so damn hard for ungrateful ass corporate America. I'll be working for me, and on my own terms. I want to be the head and not the tail. I hope one day to be financially secure to provide for the welfare of my family and be able to provide assistance to benefit my favorite charity, community care, elderly care, and advocacy for children without it being a financial burden on me. Sure, I give back some on what I make now, but there's so much more I would like to do. One of my dreams is to be able to help people who need it. I love helping people. I just want to be able to give back and it not be a financial strain on my family's needs though," Bria said.

"Sounds like you're reaching your breaking point with that place, and as far as me being tired of hearing it, no I'm not. I would rather you vent to me anytime than to keep all that bottled up in you," Harmony said.

"Believe me, Harm, I've reached my breaking point, and I'm done fighting for something that will never happen there. It's useless, and I believe God has a better plan for me. Working at the plant and with some of the individuals I've had to deal with has made me see things in a different light. This day and age, I find myself asking what Coretta and Martin would think if they were here. Sometimes it doesn't seem like much has changed, has it? Is this what they stood for? I mean, am I supposed to just stand by and watch how unfair we as black folks get treated on my job? I don't think so. Where's the justice? It just isn't fair. If I say something, I'm called an angry black woman, or I'm trying to use the race card. I know that's not the case. I don't want anything that I don't work hard to get. I see so much unfairness on a day-to-day basis—too much to even go into," Bria said.

"Girl, you know we've both been through hell and high water, so I know whatever you decide you'll come out alright."

"Thanks for having faith in me, friend. You can bet, I'll no longer be sitting around feeling sorry for myself while life passes me by or foolishly waiting for that pie in the sky. Oh no, that isn't happening. I've finally realized if I want something different to happen in my life, then I'm going to have to change what I'm doing to get new results. It's like wanting to lose weight to look fine as Janet Jackson but not putting in the work. You and I know Janet was a pudgy little girl. You don't have a body like that without walking, exercising, sweating, and eating right. How do you expect to have a six-pack when you do nothing to achieve those weight goals? You can want, want and want things to be different but without putting forth any effort, it's a waste of time...am I right?" Bria said.

"I hear you, girl. It's so damn hard. I mean you and I both listen to Oprah and that damn Steve Harvey radio show. Even Bishop T. D. Jakes talks about finding your passion and repositioning yourself. Oprah's butt even has the nerve to say you can just quit your job and do whatever the hell your passion is. Yeah, right. That's easier said than done. If I do that I'd be sitting at the Rescue Mission." Harmony responded.

"Harm, Oprah's ass won't be sitting at the Rescue Mission with you, but ole girl will throw you some money to keep the doors open for you. You know she's good about helping folks in need though, so I ain't mad at her. All I'm saying is this: I have dreams too. It's time to act on those dreams. I just know what I've been doing isn't working. All I've been hearing is if you keep doing what you've been doing, you'll keep getting what you've been getting. I want to do something different to see if that philosophy works.

"So now, back to your question. I just have this burning sensation inside me that there's more. At least now, I know I have something to work toward. I'll chat with you later, girlfriend," Bria said.

"Okay, girlfriend. Hang in there. Remember our pact though: Whichever one of us makes it big first looks out for the other one," Harmony said.

"Girl, I've got your back. You know that," Bria said.

"I've got yours too. Talk later," Harmony said.

Talking with Harmony always felt good, and Bria knew it was the therapy she needed to help her sort things out. She and Harmony had the type of relationship where they could discuss anything with each other without judgment. The one thing that kept crossing her mind was whether to leave Rockford or continue to stay. In the past, one of the major factors for her was uprooting her children and leaving Bea. But now that the children were grown, Bria felt now was the time.

Neither idea seemed reasonable to her, and she felt selfish for even considering leaving because she felt a responsibility to be near her mother. Since Bea was getting up in age, Bria was concerned about relocating Bea from familiar surroundings.

She always knew that if she were to leave Rockford, it was a given Bea should go along too. For one thing, Bria had been facing the prospect of placing Bea in an elderly assisted living environment or nursing home facility. Second, there was the issue of her job, which she sometimes loathed and despised, but knew she needed for financial security. Finally, the children.

When the children were younger, it seemed too hard to have them start over in new schools and so on. Then there was the fear of the unknown, even for her. She just didn't know if she was ready to sacrifice the familiarity of hers and the children's life by moving to a new place and starting over from scratch at that stage in her life, so she'd foregone relocating and remained in Rockford.

Bria had used many reasons to stay stagnant and hadn't realized how much time had passed until the divorce from Rad was final. That's when reality started to set in. Recognizing that there was still a void and that she yearned for more, and suddenly realizing how fast life was oozing past her, it was as if she was finally getting it.

What she lacked—what she needed—was to focus on her personal value. She went back to school, determined to win the prize this time. After several months of making headway while working relentlessly, she withdrew. This time the excuse was because she had, after several attempts, finally been offered a management position within the company. Initially hired on in the clerical bargaining union, she had been with the company several years before getting the opportunity she felt she deserved. When she was in the union, she had received several promotions up the ranks because of placement on the seniority list based on the company's contractual bargaining agreement process.

One of her Hispanic co-workers had said to her one day during work that anyone who was promoted to an entry-level management position at the company was just in a glorified clerical position and that she would never want to work in management. Bria considered the source because she knew this girl did only enough to get by, and had it not been for the union, she would have lost her job years ago. Bria saw how the girl would play the system. So, when the girl made that comment, it came as no surprise to her. She recalled one of their last conversations.

"I'm not knocking being in the union. I'm grateful. The pay is good, but I'm a bit bored with my job. I just need to do something a bit more challenging than answering a phone and doing this redundant data entry. Most of what we do, we don't even think— basically, the same calls day in and day out," Bria said.

"Well, I don't want to be in management. You become a flunky for the company. I'm no kiss-ass person. I do what I want when I want. I have too much seniority for them to try to get rid of me. Anyhow, I love talking to people and helping people through their issues," her co-worker Marciella Ramirez replied.

"I like helping people too. That's why I volunteer at church. Not quite the same as 'why is my bill so high,' or some of the other account inquiries we get from our customers in this call center. Okay, Marciella, so don't go discouraging me because I apply for a management position and you don't. If you're happy with being a senior customer service representative, I'm happy for you. I just feel I need more alright, that's all I'm saying," Bria said.

Bria was promoted to management within the same company after years of trying and many rejection letters. She was quite elated upon being offered her first entry-level management position. Between home, the new job, and school, things soon got overwhelming, and Bria decided to withdraw from school for a while. But as time passed, Bria realized she still wanted more than just a management job. She knew she wanted a career and needed to feel passionate about her work.

She had initially believed the entry-level role would lead to future opportunities and was excited about that. She later heard through the rumor mill that she was the lowest paid and got the worst assignments. She tried to ignore the gossip and focus on her goals. She could keep it going for so long until she started noticing the difference in treatment from some of the higher-level white bosses and her white colleagues. Some of it was hidden but most of it was blatant and egregious but she did not want to use the race card for fear of retaliation, so she continued to do her job but made a mental note that she had to figure out what to do next.

There were times when she felt she was put in the position because they needed a minority and she just happened to be in the right place at the right time. Whatever the case, she intended to make it work to her benefit regardless what others thought about the situation. As ironic as it was, her faith in God encouraged her to make the best of it and use the opportunity as résumé building if nothing else.

Faith—and lots of it—was a good thing for her to have as she would soon learn. She had again used her fantasy to dream up a management world full of helpful individuals all working together as a team for one motive: the success of the company. Quite to the contrary. Instead, what she found was management peers attacking her work, higher management attacking her for fear of their superiors and the constant backlash from the union individuals she now worked with. Bria was tired of the constant mind-game playing and decided after working at the utility company for twenty-plus years, it was time out for that.

Bria was one of the first African-American females ever promoted to management from the union at the company during the early eighties But this, too, was unacknowledged by management, HR or anyone of significance at the company but Bria and some of her fellow black counterparts knew it was a fact. But like so many other disparities within that place, it wasn't worth making a big deal about. The company was incorporating all the other cultures to support their newfound culturally diverse company and Bria along with her black peers were tired of fighting.

In Bria's opinion, ConEd Power Company in the little rural town was still light-years away from the rest of the world. Bria found herself constantly struggling with what had been her life-long dream of being an entrepreneur starting her own business but had not been financially able to pursue taking the risk or rather was afraid too for fear of failure. As she thought about it, as she often did, things would have been different if it was just her, but she could not risk having a dependable and good income for fear it could put the livelihood of her family at stake, so she settled for the safer route and took the position at the utility company, believing it would provide an opportunity for career advancement, which ultimately she hoped would give her the level of financial security she needed to be able to provide for her family.

Unfortunately, it became clearer and clearer to her what she must do in order to maintain her dignity and sanity. The white male–oriented environment dominated her world, which she had once thought would make all the difference in her life and in which she worked so hard to attain her personal career goals and success had proven to be mentally challenging and physically stressful. Metaphorically speaking, she would relentlessly ensure all bases were covered so she wouldn't be caught in the office landmines where certain individuals meticulously set traps to cause her career doom. She was beginning to question whether it was all worth the struggle. Her faith had strengthened her. She was determined to excel and refused to give in to what seemed like a never-ending battle, so she continued to fight for what she wanted.

There were times she wanted to literally scream when her boss Emil Celzior would confront her with office-related incidents from the union staff. She vividly recalled an incident she had etched in her mind and wouldn't forget.

"So, what do you see as the scheduling issues, and what can we do to improve the issues that the operators are having?" Emil asked.

Bria thought carefully before responding, knowing Emil would have been caught off guard and found it out of her character to say exactly what she was thinking. *What damn issues?*

What about all games they play and unnecessary stress they cause me? How about you all start managing these high-paid baby boys and standing up for what's right instead of wiping grown men's asses, she thought, knowing she would never be that disrespectful to say it out loud.

Instead, Bria responded as professionally as she could with a concerned look and hoped her facial expression didn't reveal her private thoughts.

"You know, Emil, I have given it lots of thought, and I think perhaps I should come in early and meet the guys as they are turning over shifts so I can personally ask them their opinions. Let's see if we can't get to the bottom of some changing shifts. Maybe that will minimize some of these issues. My objective is to engage the worker and ensure the best overall outcome for the individual and for the company," Bria said.

Bria could feel her calves tightening, a habit she had acquired over the years when she was under tense situations.

"Yes, I agree, Bria. I was thinking perhaps we should put your office back out in the plant with the guys so they're able to reach you during the day. By the way, Jesse Slaughter said he was bypassed on the callout list and that he should be offered makeup overtime and callout pay for it. Gip Whiner sent an email to Mr. Plezevbo referring to overtime. He should have received callout pay for the overtime that Edgar Compliner worked on May 12. Do you have any insight on these claims?"

Again, calves clinching, Bria thought before responding, *Give 'em whatever the hell they want. What you need to do is stand up and be a manager and stop letting them manage you.* Instead she replied in a professional tone, "I will check the past overtime and callout list, Emil, and research this matter and get back with you once I've gathered all the facts. Possibly this was an oversight. I won't know for sure until I research these issues further. Were there any other matters that we need to discuss? I have a one o'clock meeting with Alex Smardoza out in the training offices."

"No. I believe that's all. Oh yes, there's one other thing: It might be a good idea for you to start keeping a ledger of events as they come up so we can track any improvements you may want to make to scheduling along the way. These ledger entries would also be helpful to you at your end-of-the-year performance review. Keeping a log is both beneficial to you and helpful to us all when going back and tracking some of the issues as they come up, you know, just so we have a flow path of how things weigh out...a way to measure your improvements," Emil said.

"Yes, I agree, Emil. I've already started keeping such a ledger," Bria responded, but thought, *You must really think I'm stupid. With all the bull going on around here, you think for a second I wouldn't keep some sort of documentation of my own accord? Bea didn't raise no fool.*

It was meetings such as those with Emil Celzior that gave her the incentive and drive she needed to make time to continue school and hopefully one day complete it. She always felt she had to have her back covered dealing with these men in that environment. It had gotten to the point where she didn't trust any of them.

Chapter Twelve

THE NEXT MORNING, BRIA WAS getting ready for work. It was Friday, and she couldn't wait for the weekend to begin so she could get a reprieve from her stressful job. In her opinion, the position itself was easy, and she felt accomplished to be in management because she believed it was a stepping stone to future higher-level achievements.

But she soon realized the challenges that came along with it. There was a lot of pettiness, game playing, and downright backstabbing in the office as it related to management versus union individuals. Bria knew she had too much to deal with at home, so she tried not to let her personal matters from her life interfere with work. Day in and day out resulted in undue mental challenges. So much so that she was mentally exhausted by the end of the week and anxious to get away from the plant for what she felt was much-needed time off.

Walking the long mile back over to the administrative offices of the building, Bria could feel the vibration of her Blackberry cell phone. The phone's screen illuminated and displayed digits she recognized were Harmony's number. She awkwardly tussled and shifted her bags as she answered the phone.

"Hey, girl. I'm just now on my way out of here. Everything okay?"

"Yeah. I was just checking with you to see what time you and the girls were going to be at Applebee's," Harmony said.

"I originally planned to be there by six, but since I'm running late getting out of here, it will be closer to six-thirty. Why? What's up?" Bria asked.

"I got done sooner than I thought, so Tia and I can meet you all there."

"Okay then, good...see you in a few." Bria flipped the phone shut and stuck it back in her purse.

Bria reached the steel fire door and started down the stairs to the third floor to exit the building using the back staircase. She walked down the long hall of the third floor, which reminded her of the white walls like an insane asylum. She began to imagine what it felt like being in a straitjacket. The brightness of the floors and the walls illuminated such that the glare from the white paint caused her to squint.

Lord, you know I need my job, and I know weeping may endure for a night, but how long is the night? Bria thought. She had been thinking about her job a lot lately. She wondered as she often did what she could have achieved had she gone to college the traditional way, completed her education sooner and attained a degree.

Bria always considered herself a hard worker and would go the extra mile as it related to getting her job done. She always stayed late and came in early. She did whatever it took to prove herself to her white counterparts, but seldom did she get the recognition she deserved. She recalled a conversation she had with one of her white co-workers, Sam Pierce. Bria thought Sam seemed like a genuine down-to-earth guy. He and Bria would often talk about work-related issues, but she made it a habit not to discuss religion or politics with Sam because she would over-hear conversations he had with others and knew her opinions differed tremendously, so, to avoid that type of confrontation in the workplace, she opted out.

But the one thing she recalled about Sam was he even ob-served how she would allow fellow colleagues to "step on her" as he put it. Sam told Bria she needed to speak up for herself and to stop being so passive. Sam's comments took her by sur-prise. She argued she was being politically correct in the work-place and not necessarily passive, but looking back over certain situations, she saw where she could have been more aggressive. Bria had known her upbringing had a lot to do with how she dealt with things. She always took the passive-aggressive ap-proach.

The conclusion she made from that point on was to do some self-evaluating. She understood the past could not be undone, but going forward, things would be different. She would see to it. She looked forward to having dinner with her daughters and was even more excited Harmony and Tia would be joining them. She thought maybe they all could enjoy a carefree evening together to take her mind off work as well as what was going on at home.

was even more excited Harmony and Tia would be joining them. She thought maybe they all could enjoy a carefree evening together to take her mind off work as well as what was going on at home.

Chapter Thirteen

BRIA FELT EXASPERATED BY THE time the day ended. She got into her car and said aloud, "Free at last. Thank you, Lord. I made it another day." No sooner than she started to pull out the parking lot, she was startled by the vibrating of her phone. She searched inside of her purse.

"Hello."

"Mom, where are you?" It was India.

"I'm just leaving prison and on my way to get you and Shea. Why? What's up?"

"Was Shea supposed to meet us here at home, or meet us there?"

"What?" Bria asked, surprised. "She should have been done

with basketball practice, showered and dressed and at home by now. So you're telling me she's not there yet?"

"No. She called and said she had to meet with the coach after practice and that she would be home later, but I thought I heard her say she was meeting us here so we could all ride together. I can't remember what Shea said. She's always lying. The phone clicked and another call came through so I just hung up on her."

"Well, I guess since I'm not a mind reader, I'll never know what's what. All I know is Shea knew we all had plans tonight. She was supposed to have her behind at home by the time I got there so we could all get to the restaurant by six-thirty. Damn. I don't know what the hell that girl is thinking about these days."

"Well, she's not here yet. Are you almost here?"

"I'm near the intersection of Halsted and Riverside. All I know is if her butt isn't there by the time I get there, then she's as good as left because I'm not wasting my time waiting on Shea tonight."

"I don't think she really cares about whether we wait on her. Wake up, Mom. Shea is doing her own thing," India said.

"Yeah, well, her doing her own thing is inacceptable. She's still a child and living in under my roof. I have too much to be dealing with than to be putting up with a teenager who doesn't know her butt from a hole in the ground," Bria said.

So much had been going on all at one time. Bria had been noticing a change in Bea's behavior lately and had wanted to share it with the children and Harmony over dinner. Cousin Elaine had phoned Bria earlier that day to say that Bea had asked for a ride to the bank and had withdrew all her money out. A few Bria had stopped by Bea's and she said she had lost her money and hadn't paid her rent. Bria didn't know what to make of her mother's actions.

By the end of the conversation with India Bria couldn't take anymore and was mentally exhausted. She pulled up to her house just seconds after she flipped shut the cell phone. She honked the horn for India to come out.

Distracted by the appearance of both her daughters coming out of the house, she jerked the wheel, not realizing her reflexes had caused her to inadvertently accelerate the pedal instead of the brake.

"Mom," India shrieked.

"Oh noooo," Shea screamed.

The noise of metal to metal was simultaneous and loud as Bria propelled into the closed garage door. She barely heard the girls. Bria thought she could hear voices in the distance. As she opened her eyes, her hands were clenched to the wheel. She felt pressure in her chest and realized she had ran the car into the garage. Seeing what had happened, a wave of emotion flooded her, and she was suddenly faced with the reality of things. All at once, Bria began to scream and cry with balled fists, beating the wheel of the car.

"No, no, no. I don't have money for this shit. No, no, no."

India and Shea tried to open the passenger door of the vehicle, calling out to their mother.

"Mom, the door is locked. Open the door. Can you get out? Mom, are you alright! Talk to us, Mom. Mom," India screamed.

Frustrated and in pain, she tried to move but realized she couldn't, so she sat still and continued to sob. At that moment, it seemed as if her world came crashing in both mentally and physically. Bria fought to regain her composure and stop crying when she heard Shea and India's voices. She did not want the girls to be any more alarmed than they already were.

"Just call 911. I'm okay," Bria managed to say.

After arriving at the hospital, Bria lay in the cold emergency room on a narrow bed flat on her back. The hospital emergency room staff had been in and out of the room performing a series of routine tests and found no broken bones or fractures. India had called Harmony immediately after calling the paramedics, so Harmony had rushed to be by her friend's side and to be sure India and Shea were okay. Afterward, Harmony made sure there were no serious issues with Bria and stayed with her to make sure the emergency room staff checked out that she was good to go.

"This too shall pass," Harmony remarked, sitting on the edge of the hospital bed.

"Girl, I'm just so tired. When I saw Shea walk out that house, something just went all over me. I had just spoken with India, and she said Shea was still at her basketball practice and not home yet, so how in the world did she get home so fast? I was just so angry when I saw her that my first reaction was to confront her. I guess I was thinking of getting out of the car without realizing I needed to put it in park first. I guess I must have gone blank and accelerated the gas pedal. I must have been thinking I was walking. It all happened so fast. What in the world is going on?" Bria asked.

"Don't worry yourself about it now, Bria. You'll get through this. I'm just glad you're okay. Sounds like you just need to take some Tylenol for the pain and you'll be fine," Harmony said.

"Yep. They ran enough tests, so nothing is broken. I'm just sore, and I'm mentally drained, but I'll live. Harm, you're my friend, so I feel I can be honest with you. I don't know if I can get through this. I seem to be going through too much all at one time. I have to contend with the stuff happening in my work life that I'm not happy with. Now, to compound the matter, I have to figure out how I'm going to repair my garage and my car. What's next?" Bria asked.

"Bri, no need for you to worry about it. Your insurance will take care of all this. That's why we pay so much for it," Harmony said.

"Right. As if I didn't already have enough bills, now I have to pay an insurance deductible for my car and home insurance to have both repaired, and up goes my insurance premiums because it was my fault, if they don't drop me after this incident. Yeah, you are right, that's why we paid insurance, and so whatever, I guess it could have been worse.

"Get dressed, girl. I'll be right outside the room. I'll let the girls know everything is alright."

"Is Shea out there?"

"Of course. Why do you ask?" Harmony sounded confused.

"Because I don't think I'm ready to see her yet. My head hurts so bad, and if I see my child right now, I believe it will only hurt worst," Bria said.

"Wait a minute, Bri. Now you know I'm your girl, but Shea is your daughter, and right now you have to think about more than just you. Your shutting her out is not the thing to do. She's going through a lot. You still have to love that child no matter what," Harmony said.

"Harm, I'm so sick of folks telling me I have to love that child. What about me? Does anyone give a damn about me and what I feel right now? I've spent my whole life living for other people. I work at a place I hate. Sure, the money is good—it pays the bills, it affords us a nice place to live. I've gotten myself in debt trying to buy things for my children I couldn't afford because I wanted them to have things I never had as a child. I've sent them to the best schools, tried to live in a decent neighborhood. For what? Where's the gratitude? India comes up pregnant at sixteen, Zach sometimes acts like he doesn't have a care in the world, and now Shea. At the end of the day, they all do whatever the hell they want to do. It fazes none of them in the least what I feel."

"So Bri, tell me this: Did you do all those things for your children because you wanted them to be the individuals you wanted them to be, or did you do all those things for your children because you loved them? Another thing to think about, girlfriend. I can't judge you since I've made my own share of mistakes. You and I both know love isn't wrapped up in what kind of house or neighborhood our kids live in. Love is the nurturing and caring for our children no matter where we live or what we have. We were young, Bri. No one ever shared that with us, but we know that now. We can't go on living in the past," Harmony said.

"What the hell are you trying to say, Harmony? You know damn well I love my children. It just makes me feel so bad to see my kids make some of the same mistakes I did, you know what I saying? It makes me wonder where did I go wrong. I thought I was there for them. I tried to get Zach to go to college, but he didn't want to go 'cause he thought it was too hard. India made her life more difficult because she was a teenage mom, just like me. I tried to prevent her from going down that road 'cause I knew firsthand what the outcome would be, so look what's happened. She will have to go through life fending for herself and a child alone.

"Harm, you and I both know that baby's daddy ain't worth a damn. He won't be there for India and her child. It's like it was a curse or something. I wanted so much better for them, that's all I'm trying to say. I'm their mother, it's my job to teach Zach, India, and Shea how to be responsible and sustainable adults. I feel I haven't done my job as a parent. Yes, I know there are things each of them will have to face that I won't be able to protect them from. I've always tried to shield and protect my children, but it's gotten to where I've lost myself in the process. I've got to learn to let go. There's only so much a parent can do, and I've got to stop beating myself up about the past. I've delayed my own happiness. I'll always be here for them, but I've got to find me. I was a mess. Now I'm free and ready to be the best me I can be," Bria said.

"Girl, I agree. Get over it. We've been friends too long for me not to be able to tell you this. You've got to let that nonsense go. You're right, as a parent, you can only do so much—teach your kids right from wrong, be a good example, provide a good home environment, convey to them the importance of a good education, give the instructions they need to be good and moral individuals to be able to exist in society. That's about all you can do. Hell, the way I see it, you're a failure when you haven't done those things, but you did encourage them., I know you did, you know it, and so do they. Still, at the end of the day, they're no different from us and what our parents tried to teach us. They have their own minds. They're free agents—free to make their own choices, good and bad, and guess what, girlfriend? They have to live with the consequences of their actions," Harmony said.

"I know it hurts, but we hurt our parents when we didn't do what they wanted us to do, but our folks didn't wallow in pain and shame and stop living. Neither should you or I. Listen, I know it sounds like an old cliché, but life goes on. Your kids are practically grown, Bria. You've done a good job. Did you forget how you picked yourself up after you and Rad divorced? You went back to school… You had been talking about it for so long. Do you know how much I admired you for that? You inspired me to go back to school. Now look how far you've come. You can do whatever you want to do. I know you. When you put your mind to it, you get it done. Go on and do the things that make you happy, but in the process, you're still a parent. Love your-self and love your children. Go on. You can do this, girl. Don't quit on me now. Please, girl, I need you too much," Harmony said.

Embracing, the two friends were brought to tears. Harmony, without saying any additional words, comforted her friend, and the two women sat on the hospital bed in silence. Harmony drew back from Bria, taking her hands in her own, looking Bria directly in the eyes.

"Bria, I have one last thing to say: I know you've already talked to Shea, but did you let her know that whatever she chooses to be in terms of her sexual identity that you are there for her and that you love and support her? Let me say this to you as your friend: Whether Shea is gay or not isn't the issue. She's still your daughter. I know I sound like a broken record, but I can't stress that enough. You've let her know you're there for her no matter what. This has gone on too long. Look, before things get any worse, don't shut your daughter out. Please promise me you will talk to her openly, and most importantly let her know you love her," Harmony said.

"I don't know what I was thinking. I guess I wasn't. This has been so hard, but you're right. I don't want to be one of those parents who disowns my child for their lifestyle. I would never want to do that. I'm here for her—for all of them. No matter what, we're family 'til the end," Bria said.

For too long Bria had been living her life in the shadows of others. Bea's alcoholism had always been the driving force that pushed her to want more in life. India's teenage pregnancy pushed her to want to break a family curse of single mothers who always seemed to live from paycheck to paycheck struggling with children. Bria constantly blamed herself for the bad choices her family members made. Not really taking the time to know herself, she constantly allowed her life to be driven by others. She asked herself what it would take to let this stuff go and begin to really focus on her needs and some of the things that made her happy.

For so long, Sabria Hudson lacked the courage to deal with some of the things in her life from her past. After Bria's marriage ended, she had been on a self-discovery mission and had decided to reach out to her father for closure among other things to try and understand why he hadn't been around. Dealing with her birth father had begun a for her a path to close what she saw as a hole in her life. Meeting him helped her understand who she was and gave her a sense of wholeness, and without him in her life, she felt incomplete, but she hadn't admitted it. She had come to learn just by talking with him they had so much in common, She was hot tempered, so was he; she was stubborn, so was he; she loved cheeseburgers, so did he. She was comforted in knowing and even understanding who she was. She had a newfound confidence in herself and felt proud for once. She admired Lee Cox. There were times when he would talk to her as if she was his long-lost friend. He was, in her opinion, so smart and intelligent. She guessed it was his way of making up for lost time, but whatever it was, she was glad to have had that time with him.

The take-away Bria got from her past was to be thankful for what was and not to be afraid to take risks in life to be successful. She would no longer talk about doing something different. This time she would actually do something different. Bria knew she had to act now and would no longer hold on to past hurt, pain, and regret. She resolved to finally accept the people in her life for who they were and not based on her expectations of who she thought they should be.

She thought how glad she was that she had decided to call Lee and that it hadn't turned out as bad as she had thought. She was shocked to find out he had wanted to reach out to her all along but did not have the courage to do so, as he put it. The two of them had talked for hours on the phone as if they were old friends getting reacquainted. She felt fortunate and relieved at the same time.

Lee had shared information about his family with her—new family she was eager to meet. Bria invited Lee over to meet the children, and they all had dinner. It was somewhat strange, but everyone seemed to welcome him as he did them. She had decided to take one day at a time and accept the present for what it was, not having any expectations on how things or the relationship would end up, but to her surprise, things were going well.

She saw a different man in Lee now that she knew he was her father. He had grown old and feeble, so she decided to forgive him and let go instead of inflicting her anguish and pain on him. After seeing him, it appeared Father Time had already taken a toll on Lee, he was a widower, so she never said what she thought she would to him to his face nor did she blame him for not being there for her, or ask any of the questions she had for him.

She felt his genuine sincerity by the way he talked with her, and in their parting ways, he always told her he loved her, and she eventually would tell him. She was glad to have finally met him. It felt good to forgive and let go and not have to waste any more negative energy on the past as it related to not having a father. Now her focus would be well spent to invest in her. Perhaps that was why she lacked so much emotionally, because she was worrying too much about others. Not anymore.

Bria believed she was fortunate to have had the opportunity to get to know her biological dad; it was a void she needed filled and realized in every case some situations did not turn out so good when an abandoned child meets the parent. But for whatever reason hers turned out remarkably well and for that she was eternally thankful.

Lee Cox died unexpectedly two years after their meeting. She appreciated Lee and enjoyed the time they spent together. The two had become almost inseparable during those couple of years, they attended church together, had dinner dates, and other social outings, she was proud to accompany him on many occasions. Lee had even taken the liberty to introduce Bria and the kids to his family. Bria thought how befitting it was to be front and center at his service, to be recognized as a member of his family, his daughter, she thought, who would have ever known this day would come.

While she didn't like it, she decided to accept the things she had no control over—Bea's alcoholism, Zach's hidden aggression due to not having his father around, India's dealing with the consequences of her teenage pregnancy, and Shea's sexuality. Bria knew she had her own share of character defects to deal with and was determined to begin a process of healing herself. She had decided to get to know herself before it was too late and to learn to move on and let the people around her learn from their own choices. She loved them and was not giving up on them, but she loved herself first and felt like she had been lost being so consumed in their lives. She had taught them right from wrong. She would ensure each of them knew how to get the most out of life but in the end it would be left up to them to get it for themselves.

Things had not been perfect along the way, but Bria felt she had provided a stable home and had taught them the value of hard work, a good education, and perseverance. She would no longer consume herself with whether they chose to do things completely her way. When they wanted her help, she would be there for them as a guide not an enabler.

She had watched too many of her single-mother friends, especially the ones who were raising sons wreak unintentional havoc on their boys lives. She had watched how they spoiled them with too many material things to occupy space or over compensate for the absent father when they were little. As a result, when the young males grew older, they would crave larger toys—by any means necessary.

She watched how her friends would cry and suffer when some of their sons ended up in jail. She realized they should have held back on some of the expensive clothes they usually couldn't afford anyhow and found a good male role model for them instead. She knew some of her girlfriends purposely kept their boys from their fathers for various reasons, but they should have at least found a substitute for the absent father—someone who could have taught them understanding from a male perspective, home skills, how to treat women with respect and just some of the things that make a young man a man.

She was sure these women didn't mean to cripple the young men like they did, but commonly she knew they were just like her—mothers who thought if they gave their children the material things they longed for, it wouldn't look like they were failures to those looking in from the outside. Surely if the kids were dressed nice and had everything, then anyone peering in would know they had a good hardworking mother who kept them out of poverty. The mother was actually trying to make herself look good, not knowing she couldn't have been more wrong.

An alternative would have been not to give children everything they wanted but to instill the value of earning the little extras a child yearns for. That's how she learned from her own mother. All the while, she thought she had such a traumatic upbringing when in fact she learned a great deal about moral living and good character just by the fact that she didn't have everything easily given to her. She had to work hard and even fight most of the time for what she wanted. It wasn't easy at all, so she wondered why some parents, especially single mothers thought kids should have it easy.

Bria had been released from the emergency room and home for a couple of days. The girls had been taking care of her, making sure she had everything she needed, preparing her food, taking care of the housekeeping and ensuring peace and quiet around the house.

Shea was the first to peek into her bedroom to break the silence. She eased the cracked door opened to find her mom sitting up in bed. Shea decided to step inside and sat crossed legged at the foot of the bed.

"Mom, I hope you're feeling better. That was a pretty close call. You really scared us. I don't know what I would have done if something had happened to you, like you know..." Shea said.

"Oh, you would have been alright, Shea, but like you, I'm glad it wasn't any worse than it was. If anything, my pride is hurt. I'm more embarrassed than anything. We can get that garage fixed. The older I get, I don't need any damage to my bones. That would be kind of hard to repair," Bria said.

"Yeah, I hear old bones take a long time to heal," Shea said.

"Who are you calling old, child? Like Bea used to say, don't nothing get old but clothes," Bria said.

The two shared a laugh.

Bria looked at Shea and saw the tenderness and sincerity in her younger daughter. She loved all her children for their individual qualities. Shea was always the most open and seemingly more giving of the three. It was hard for anyone not to embrace her kindness and love for people. She was not judgmental and openly disapproved of others' lack of caring toward individuals. Bria would always use these one-on-one times spent with her children as opportunities to get closer to them and embrace what they were thinking and how each one of them thought. So being upfront and not wanting to beat around the bush any longer, she mustered up the courage to begin her conversation.

"So Shea, I know we had this conversation before. I asked you if you are gay, you said nawww. Maybe it's the labeling you don't like. I need you to know you can be open with me. I'm your mother. I love you no matter what. Are you gay?" Bria asked.

"I wouldn't call it that, Mom. I'm still attracted to guys too. I know who I am. Whether you call it gay or whatever, I have a friend who happens to be a girl who I like. We do things together, we talk, and we have fun," Shea said.

"It's Chelsea, isn't it? I don't understand. Is this just a fad, or do you think you're in love with her because I know it's been going on for a while? I should have said something about this a while ago when I first noticed a change in your behavior. figure you've been covering this up for a while. I have to be honest with you: I knew you were different. I just didn't want to admit it. But whether you like labels or not, the way I see it is this: when girls like girls and boys like boys, that's called gay. So you are gay, that's just it. Get ready for the labels, honey. There are so many horrible labels, dyke, bull dagger, lesbian, butch... society will be much rougher on you than I am. I just want you to be ready for what happens on the outside and the ostracizing that comes with the lifestyle you have chosen, " Bria asked.

"Mom, you're right. You really don't have to put a label on it. Like I said, I just like who I like, and I'm comfortable with it. Please don't judge me on this. See, that's why I wasn't upfront with you. I didn't judge you when you and my dad went through what you did. You knew he was seeing that woman and had that baby while you were married, and you even knew he was using drugs and wasn't helping you much with things around the house, but you kept on giving him chances. I didn't judge you. I thought some of it was crazy, but I just felt you loved him and would get tired of it and do different when you were ready. I still love you and him, even though I hated the situation. It was hard for me to get over him doing you and us the way he did, but I learned to separate him being my dad from him being your husband and the person who did you wrong.

"Mom, sometimes you just have to let people be themselves. I can't live my life based on how you want me to live, but that doesn't make me any more or less a good human being. I just wish people would stop treating people cruelly because of life-style choices. Some people like to treat us like we're freaks of nature or something just because we're not the so-called norm. I'm not a freak, Mom. I have feelings too, so please stop treating me that way," Shea said.

"Baby, I'm sorry if I've been treating you like a freak. By no means do I think you are. It's just that I love you so much. I know how society treats people when we are different, I was just trying to protect you from getting hurt, that's all. I'm your mother. Please try and understand where I'm coming from. I worry something bad will happen to you, like you'll be ridiculed or bullied. I don't want anyone to treat you mean because you're gay. Maybe I'm being ignorant, I don't know. I just worry about you so much. Are you sure you're ready for these types of things in life? Not only that. I know there's AIDS to consider."

"Oh my God, Mom. It's not that serious. Are you kidding me?" Shea said, frowning at her mom in disbelief at what she had just heard.

"Don't look at me like that. Maybe that was too extreme to say, but my point is whether you're with a woman or man, you have to consider sexually transmitted diseases. Look at what happened to Uncle Earl. Our family walked around his lifestyle like it was the elephant in the room. No one acknowledged his homosexuality or the fact he was gay until he got sick, and even then Bea denied it. I know for a fact how he died because I happened to stumble on the medical records in the emergency room on one of his visits prior to his death.

"Uncle Earl died from AIDs, Shea, I don't want to pretend like stuff like that isn't real. Like I said, I'm your mother. I would be doing you a disservice not to talk to you about the concerns I have. I hate I wasn't able to approach you about this sooner.

"I wonder too, did anything happen to you when you were younger. Did it, Shea? Did anyone ever molest you? You can tell me. If anyone ever harmed you in any way, please let me know. It's not too late to get help. Did anyone in our family or a stranger for that matter touch you inappropriately? It would hurt, but please, I have to know," Bria said.

"Mom, you can bet that no one touched me. I wasn't molested. I've always known I was this way. It isn't anyone's fault. I know you don't understand, but I'm fine. I just like who I like and want to be with who I want to be with. I'm not a drug addict, I'm not illiterate, I'm not stupid, I'm not an alcoholic, I don't sleep around. I feel I am perfectly normal," Shea said.

"*Hmmph,* I don't know about perfectly normal. That just doesn't seem normal to me at all. I can't say that right away I'm going to be okay with this because honestly, I'm not. I will say that I'll try to understand. I do love you. There's no doubt about that. Now, I have to say this: Be it girl or boy, I don't want any premarital sex of any kind in my house or for that matter you, India, and Zac should all abstain until...well we know India didn't, but still, I have to let you know I don't condone premarital sex, no matter what mistakes we've seen in the past," Bria said.

"Mom, I got that. I just need you to stop treating me like some sort of freak," Shea said.

"Shea, like I said, I'm so sorry for that. Please forgive me. I'll try to do better... No, I will do better. I'm here for you, baby. I really am. Now, give your momma a hug," Bria said.

"Love you, Mommy," Shea said, leaning toward her mother.

"Love you more, baby."

Chapter Fourteen

BRIA FELT A LOAD LIFTED since having had the discussion with Shea about her sexuality. Bria was glad she and Shea were in a better place after talking more in depth about what had been going on in Shea's life. It had seemed like such a difficult situation to discuss for so long, and Bria knew she had to let her daughter know her honest point of view. In her mind, Bria was still trying to process it all. She found it hard, but she loved her child so much that she would always be there for her no matter what obstacle they faced.

After things settled, Bria sat down with Zach, India, and Shea to let them know about Bea. She had taken her to the doctor and had learned Bea had dementia. Her health seemed to deteriorate fast, likely due to the years of drinking along with other health issues so the physician recommended she go to a long-term nursing care facility. Bria gave it much thought after realizing how difficult it was to attempt to keep her mother at home and work full time. Bea's combativeness from the dementia made it even harder to do, so Bria would get her occasionally on the weekends. It hurt Bria to see Bea so fragile and at times nonresponsive. She was used to the feisty, sassy Bea.

The reality was Bria had for so long had a fictional concept of what the idea of family looked like. She never envisioned life without Bea. Even though things weren't perfect in her home, she had learned to accept a certain kind of normalcy with the way she had been brought up. Bria had a picture in her mind of what she saw on TV shows like *Leave it to Beaver, The Brady Bunch,* and *The Cosby Show.* ffj ese were some of the shows she grew up on and wanted to emulate. She knew all too well that was not real and was not how life was going to be, especially not in her world.

Bria had seen a lot in her lifetime, but over time, she had come to appreciate her life, her family, the brokenness in her family structure, Bea's alcoholism, growing up without a father, raising her own children without their dads, past promiscuity, insecurity, and all that made her who she was.

I'm not a bad person, she thought. *I'm okay, and I'm happy with me. I can be who I want to be.*

Bea's residency at the nursing care facility sped by, and her condition progressed for the worse. Bria remembered vividly the call she had received from the attending duty nurse to consider hospice care. In denial, Bria found it hard to accept what she had to do, but after seeing Bea in the state she was in, reality struck like a bolt of lightning. Bria was grateful Bea didn't languish long, it seemed just a matter of days before she and the kids were all in the room with Bea when she passed.

As Bria reminisced over the last few years regarding how things had changed, she began to reflect and re-evaluate life. Bea's passing was the beginning of a turning point in Bria's life. Bea looked so beautiful and peaceful, much like the woman young Bria remembered from her youth. Bria honored her mother by making sure her funeral was a tribute to her life and reflected love from her family despite any past indiscretions. At that point, Bria had no regrets. Life was what it was, and she knew shc had to deal with it.

Bea's passing gave Bria a certain epiphany, a newfound strength. Somehow in the midst of her grief, she mustered up the strength to move forward. A voice inside her said, if you can get through the death of your mother, you can do anything. For some reason she started searching the internet to get options for colleges that offered adult accelerated learning opportunities and schedules. She found a program that would take the credits she had already obtained from the years at the community college. She then enrolled in the next semester's fall classes to complete her undergraduate degree. She was actually beginning to make progress. She thought, *Baby steps. That's all it takes, one step at a time, I'll get there.*

She still found pleasure in jotting passages in her journal. While rereading her past passages, she became intrigued by some of what she wrote and how well it read.

"Follow your passion" came to mind, clear as if someone was

speaking right in front of her. She started to type the words from her journal into her computer because for the past several weeks she had been toying with the idea of developing her writing with the prospects of someday writing an affirmations book.

Bria had been writing and keeping track of small affirmations to herself for the past several weeks to help herself overcome negative and sabotaging thinking. For now, it seemed she had learned to embrace life and all its twists and turns. She appreciated her past and her present. She would no longer feel ashamed of her lineage, but she would embrace the past that helped make her the person she had become. She had learned to forgive, to love unconditionally, to accept the norms that she had come to know in her life, and to live. She realized she didn't have to remain stuck in her dysfunctional past. She made a choice to do different. She chose not to be afraid to do better and to be better.

The best teacher for her had been experience. Without it, she wouldn't be the person she was. She learned one cannot simply shut the door on one's past, but that one can learn to let go with love and to stand back—sometimes in agony, often in pain—and watch our loved ones, especially our children, make their own mistakes while she must go on living—not just existing, but really living.

That's what letting go was all about, learning to live even when it is sometimes quite painful. Thank God for allowing all the pain, keeping her through all of life's ups and downs. She smiled as she thought about Bea, Zach, India, and Shea. They may not have had life on a silver platter, but to her they had much more. They had each other, and they had love and endurance.

A few days later, Bria reached out to Harmony to meet for drinks and to catch up. Sabria Hudson possessed a new attitude and felt confidant. She was feeling at peace with life and was looking forward to meeting her friend just for some fun and much-needed girl talk. The ladies had settled in and placed their order off the menu with the waitress before starting to chat.

"Hey, girl...you're looking snazzy today," Harmony said. "I haven't seen you look this good in ages. New haircut. Love the outfit. Is that a Free People brand kimono? It really looks great with that tank and those jeans, and is that a new lip color you're wearing?"

"Why, yes, ma'am. You're quite the observant one, aren't you? Thanks. Yep. I thought I would step out of the box. You know I've been wearing that bright ass red for ages. You don't think it's too orange, do you? Anyhow, I needed to spruce it up a bit, I was beginning to feel a bit drab. The sales associate at Macy's talked me into this outfit. She said the kimono is in and has a slimming appeal to it. I guess it's working, huh?" Bria said.

"Yes, it absolutely is, girlfriend. I love that color on you, and you're anything but drab, girl. You know you always had a good fashion sense. You're working that kimono, and I guess working out at the gym has paid off too 'cause you look thinner. I see it all in your cheeks and neckline. You got a new man you're not telling me about? How are things going now that you and Shea have talked and things are out in the open?"

"Naw, girl. No man to speak of yet. That's the last thing I need right now. I'm good, but I have to say I believe things are going to be okay. It's been a rough road, but it's going to be alright. The most important thing to me is my family—all of them. Even Lee Cox. You ever think about everything we've been through?" Bria asked.

"Yeah, I do. We could write a best seller, couldn't we?" Harmony said.

"Yeah, but we had better wait until some folks die first." Bria laughed.

"Ain't that the truth? Really, you really look happy, like...I can't explain it. Whatever you're doing, it's working, friend, so keep it up," Harmony said.

"I guess that's the residual effect of relinquishing things I have no control over and focusing on what—no, should I say who—I need to focus on, and that's me. Don't get me wrong, I'm not saying I don't care about my kids, their health, happiness, and whatever, but what I'm learning is there is only so much I can do as a parent, and the rest is up to them."

"Wow, I am impressed. Is this Ms. Superwoman Sabria Twon who has to know every detail and be in control of every outcome and have the last say in every aspect of life in America? Say it ain't so," Harmony quipped.

"You better know it, girl. You're looking at a whole new person. Lately, I've been doing a lot of thinking."

After some casual chitchat, the waitress placed the food on the table.

"Okay, I'm listening. Ooh, this food is good. Go on girl, I didn't mean to interrupt," Harmony said.

"So, like I was saying, I've been doing a lot of reflecting on life and trying to put things in perspective 'cause you know we're not getting any younger, and what I've come up with is this: My life hasn't been that bad. I mean yeah, there have been some ups and downs, but then that's life. Who hasn't experienced ups and downs, right?" Bria asked.

"Uh...Yeah, so what else is new? Lord knows we've all had our share of things that have happened in our lives. Some things good and some not so good, so whatever. And whoever is walking around here thinking their life is perfect is a lie, and you and I both know it. You know I don't care what nobody says about me and mine, I'm going to keep it real. I can't stand fake folks," Harmony said.

"I know that's right, but honestly I struggled through the years always trying to please people or live a certain way. Anyhow, I'm done with all that, I understand my value and my own self-worth. I'm content with being who I am, and if nobody else does, then shame on them. I've asked myself for the last time by whose standards am I not normal. There is no normal or one right way to have a family.

"The last time I checked, everybody's family has some level of dysfunction. I even read somewhere that scientific studies have proven the most value a child can have from his or her upbringing is not having being brought up in the so-called model or mode of what society says is the family structure, such as one that included a stay-at-home mother and a breadwinning father. More importantly, the family structure is the quality of the relationship between the individuals who are caring for one another within a specific network. I say all this to say none of us ever really benefited from society's cookie-cutter classifications. Besides that, statistically speaking, most of it is bullshit—

simple B.S. That's what it is. Once people realize they have choices, they can choose any alternative to be successful in life and have healthy relationships with family."

"Alright, girl, you're getting deep up in here," Harmony said.

"I'm not trying to. You can just say I'm finally purging myself of the unnecessary stress of trying to please everyone or trying to meet someone else's expectations. Look at all the time I've wasted doing that. What I've come to realize is we're all dysfunctional in our own way, some more than others, and none of us are perfect. I lost myself. I was consumed with feelings of inadequacy all my life. I allowed men to use me because I thought I needed one to make me complete. I had given too much of who I was to the point where I did not even know myself. That, my friend, has changed. I know my self-worth and I am in a good place now," Bria said.

"I know now what I didn't before. I always thought I needed a man in my life to make it complete. I was lost focusing on the wrong thing. Now I know the real key to happiness is to begin from the inside out. I had to work on me first, get to know what my life goals are and then work on those things. The rest will come. I've made enough bad choices as it relates to men. No more Bria of the jungle, swinging from relationship to relationship. Oh no, I'm done with that, the next man will have to come looking for me. I'm good with being with me for now. I have to get me together first.

"Seriously, you have to let go of bitterness, and most of all learn to forgive. This is my truth, and I can't speak for anyone else. I have learned to let go of the past. Don't wait to prosper. Live the best you can while you can. You can spend a lifetime blaming others for your failures, I don't want to be that kind of person. I plan on embracing my right now, savoring the moment, and enjoying the ride. Life is too short for nonsense. That doesn't mean I'm about to become some happy-go-lucky free-spirited individual who runs off into the sunset and leaves family, priorities and all cares behind. What it does mean is I welcome life and whatever comes along next. I accept it and welcome the challenge to do better. I will make the best of it, whatever it is," Bria said.

"You go, girl, and you know I've got you. No matter what, I'm always here for you. We've been through hell and high water together," Harmony said.

"Soooo, for now, I've decided to make a few decisions in my life. I'm retiring from the plant. I'm taking some of my hard-earned retirement money and investing in me. You might say I'm riding off into the sunset...whatever, but I'm going to travel the world—alone. Yes, alone all by my damn self. Don't try to stop me 'cause you know when Sabria Twon makes up her mind, there's no changing it. This is just to let you know, and don't worry I'll touch base with you from time to time, but this is something I have to do.

"The last few years have been a whirlwind. The discovery of Uncle Earl's HIV/AIDs, then his death, dealing with Bea's dementia, working full time while being Bea's caregiver along with having to finally place her in the nursing home facility, her passing, my dad's sudden passing, and not to mention the regular life stuff that just occurs from day to day. Life is just too short not to be happy, and in my opinion it's now or never.

"Let's toast to living our best life. We might have been late bloomers in finding ourselves, but life's too short to live boring and vicariously. You've got to get out and live a little, and I attest you can be happy, live your dreams and have success at any age. So yeah, it was okay for me to get a degree in my mid-forties. Hell, it's alright if I decide to retire and start a business at mid-fifty. Age is nothing but a number, and it's never too late. As long as I have breath in my body, I will continue to grow, and who knows, I might even write a book one day. Here's to one thing we know for sure and two things we know for certain, love yourself, love life, work hard, and play harder. Cheers to our future. We own our destiny and our dreams, and our passions will be fulfilled," Bria said.

THE END

Book Club Discussion Questions

1. Who was your favorite character from *The Chronicles of Bria Twon* and why?
2. Who was your least favorite character and why?
3. How did Bria's relationship with her mother impact her life?
4. What is the biggest obstacle you think Bria had to overcome to have the life of which she'd always dreamed?
5. Bria dealt with lots of workplace drama. Discuss a time you've dealt with drama at work or school.
6. What's the biggest lesson you learned from the story?
7. How did Bria growing up without a father impact her life?
8. Bria's kids were her life. How do kids change your life?

About the Author

EARTHA G. GATLIN WAS BORN in Rockford, Illinois. She is the proud mother of three children, Demond, Paris, and Jasmine, and grandmother of two, Jada and JaKobe. Eartha loves the Lord, professing her faith at a young age, and transformed to the will of God as a young adult.

Eartha served others as an active member of Providence Baptist Church (PBC) in Rockford, Illinois, and previously held the following roles: young adult women's Sunday school teacher, vacation bible school director, vice president of Voices of Praise choir and member of the PBC Praise Team. Eartha also had the esteemed honor of being one of the featured speakers for the 2011 PBC Annual Women's Day program.

Eartha worked thirty-three-plus years at a Fortune 500 public utility company in Midwestern Illinois. A trailblazer in her own right, she worked her way up through the ranks, becoming one of the first African-American women within her work location to be promoted from a clerical bargaining union position to a management role overcoming various obstacles. At the age of fifty, she graduated from Judson University, Elgin in Illinois with a bachelor of arts degree in management and leadership and human resources management. She says that although studying as an adult was a sacrifice, with prayer and a lot of faith, she made the dean's list every quarter with letters to substantiate it and made it through.

Being a lifelong learner, she later earned a master of management/human resources management degree from the University of Phoenix in Arizona. After countless attempts to break the glass ceiling and racial disparity at the utility company, Eartha decided it was time to retire from corporate America.

Eartha loves learning about God's Word. She also enjoys spending time with family and friends, reading *Essence* and *O* magazines and novels, traveling, interior decorating, and shopping. Eartha felt compelled to put faith into action and leave her hometown to relocate in Dallas, Texas, to pursue a career in writing, a lifelong passion.

Eartha's vision is to live so that others, particularly disenfranchised women, young and old, will be inspired to pursue their dreams at any age. Eartha lives by the quote translated from Ecclesiastes 9:10: "Whatever you do, do well. For when you go to the grave there will be no work or planning or knowledge or wisdom."